the Gun of Jesse Hand

Center Point Large Print

**This Large Print Book carries the
Seal of Approval of N.A.V.H.**

the Gun of Jesse Hand

Lewis B. Patten

CENTER POINT PUBLISHING
THORNDIKE, MAINE

This Center Point Large Print edition
is published in the year 2009 by arrangement with
Golden West Literary Agency.

The text of this Large Print edition is unabridged.
In other aspects, this book may vary
from the original edition.
Printed in the United States of America.
Set in 16-point Times New Roman type.

ISBN: 978-1-60285-349-2

Library of Congress Cataloging-in-Publication Data

Patten, Lewis B.
  The gun of Jesse Hand / Lewis B. Patten.
     p. cm.
  ISBN 978-1-60285-349-2 (library binding : alk. paper)
  1. Large type books. I. Title.

PS3566.A79G83 2009
813'.54--dc22

2008038990

I

I CAN still remember that April day. The sky was blue for a thousand miles and the land was green for as far as the eye could see. Every now and then a meadowlark would warble and there was that unmistakable smell in the air that goes with spring. The leaves on the cottonwoods along the bed of Cottonwood Creek rustled in the breeze. A door slammed somewhere. I heard a child crying and a woman scolding it. The windmill creaked out behind the livery barn.

Old Charlie Two Horses came shuffling up Main Street and crossed the vacant lot beside the Free State Saloon, heading for the alley behind the place. A black-and-white dog ran out from the shade of the saloon and barked at his heels. Charlie went on through the lot, paying no attention to the dog. He disappeared.

I knew what he was doing in back of the saloon. He was going through the empties thrown out early that morning by Ben Simms when he cleaned out the litter of the night before. There were a few drops of whiskey left in each bottle and Charlie always drained them patiently, one by one.

Finishing, he came shuffling through the lot again, licking his lips. He squatted down against the front wall of the saloon. He closed his eyes and drowsed, soaking up the sun.

Indians weren't supposed to have whiskey and nobody would have sold it to Charlie even if he'd had the money to buy it with. But neither did anybody see harm in the few drops he got out of the empties behind the saloon every day. I didn't know how old Charlie was, but from the look of him I'd have said he was eighty at least. He'd been left on the prairie to die a long time ago by his tribe but he'd had more strength and will to live than they'd thought he had. Somebody had found him and revived him and brought him to town. Now he had a tarpaper shack on the creek a quarter-mile outside of town. He lived off scraps and whatever small animals he could snare.

This particular morning I was loading a wagon in front of Blumenthal's Mercantile where I worked. I saw the two strangers the minute they rode into town. They came from the west and they looked like they'd been on the trail a long time. Their faces were covered with whiskers and their clothes with dust. Their horses looked beat.

They gave Charlie Two Horses some pretty hard looks as they dismounted and tied their horses to the rail in front of the saloon. They did some grumbling back and forth but I couldn't make out anything they said. They went into the saloon.

I kept working and finally finished loading the wagon. I was sweating so I just stood there a minute, letting the breeze cool me off. The men had been in the saloon for more than half an hour by this time and I'd forgotten them.

Suddenly the swinging doors of the saloon slammed open and the two came out. They looked down at Charlie, scowling, and one of them kicked him as he went by, pretending he had stumbled and that it was an accident. Charlie kind of hunched down some more but he did not look up.

The two stepped into the street, untied their horses and mounted. I was feeling kind of shaky in my stomach and in my hands and knees. There had been no excuse for kicking Charlie. He hadn't done anything. But there hadn't been time for me to interfere even if I'd been foolish enough.

Coming from the west the way they had, it was understandable that the two strangers didn't like Indians. It was 1870 and the Cheyennes were still making trouble over in Colorado Territory because of the Washita fight two or three years before. They had burned ranches and attacked stage-coaches and killed some settlers.

The two strangers turned away from the hitchrail and started down the street. Suddenly one of them whirled his horse and came riding back. He rode up on the boardwalk, his horse balking and plunging, and dropped a loop over Charlie Two Horses's head. He dallied the rope and reined his horse away, yanking Charlie away from the wall, jerking and flopping around like a limp rag doll. He trotted his horse down the street, grinning back at Charlie dragging helplessly along behind. Charlie's body raised a plume of dust but he never made a sound.

Half a block down the street, the pair turned and came riding back. They spurred their horses until they were galloping. They began to yell and the one dragging Charlie was laughing like something was funny about what was happening.

I ought to have had better sense than to do what I did. I guess I got mad and I sure didn't think. Fumbling in my pocket for my knife, I ran into the street. I got it open just as the horse dragging Charlie galloped past.

Running, I slashed at the rope with my knife. I'd grabbed it with one hand and now I was dragged off my feet. In spite of that, I kept working at the rope and finally managed to cut it through.

I rolled helplessly in the dust but I held on to the knife. I got up and went back to help Charlie to his feet. It wasn't any use. Charlie Two Horses was dead. There was no movement at all in his chest.

I felt numb when I discovered that. It seemed unbelievable that a life could have been so quickly snuffed out. A minute ago Charlie had been alive. Now he was dead, killed by these two strangers for nothing more than their own amusement and killed in a way that no man should ever have to die.

I don't know what I'd have done about it if I'd had a choice. I wasn't armed except for the pocket-knife and I was only seventeen years old. I was no match for hardcases like those two. But I didn't have a choice. A rope settled over me, pinning my arms to my sides. I was yanked off my feet and dragged along the street the way Charlie had been only a few moments before. The rope cut into my upper arms. The ground shredded my shirt and pants and raked the skin off one whole side of me before I'd gone a hundred yards.

It took a few seconds for me to get over my surprise. I was hurt and shaken up but mostly I was mad. I managed to get hold of the rope with one hand and began trying to cut it with the knife that I still held in the other one. I cut my hand while I was doing it and I suppose I could have jabbed the knife blade into my face dragging along the street like that, but I didn't. The motion stopped suddenly and I realized that I had succeeded in cutting through the rope. I also realized I had better move fast before those two could stop their horses, dismount and get back to me.

I struggled to my feet. I could scarcely see because my eyes were full of dirt. My mouth was too. I'd breathed a lot of dust and it made me choke. But I was mad. Oh my God, I was mad.

I suppose I figured those two hardcases were going to beat me with their fists. Maybe I didn't even stop to think. Maybe what I did was pure instinct and nothing else. I ducked between them and ran toward their horses, my eyes fixed on their saddle guns.

The horses spooked away from me but I grabbed one of them. He kept plunging and trying to get away from me and he finally did, but not before I'd succeeded in yanking the new Spencer carbine out of the saddle boot. I levered a shell into the chamber of the gun and whirled to face the men. I'd handled a gun like this one a couple of months before in the hardware store so I knew how.

Both of them had stopped cold in their tracks. They were staring at me with open mouths. I could see they were both realizing belatedly how badly this stupid business had gotten out of hand. They knew they were going to have to kill me or die themselves. Both made frantic grabs for the revolvers they carried in holsters at their sides.

I fired and saw one of them flinch as the bullet struck. Fortunately one of the horses picked that instant to run in front of me.

That gave me time to lever in another shell and change my position a bit. The horse raised some dust running in front of me but not enough to obscure my view of the men. One of them was down on the ground. The other fired the instant the horse got out of his way.

I don't know where the bullet went. It didn't hit me and I didn't hear it, probably because the muzzle blast of the revolver was so deafening. I raised the rifle and sighted this time, and when my sights were on the second man's chest I squeezed off the trigger the way grandpa had taught me to.

The second man was driven back the way he'd have been if he'd been kicked by a mule. He flopped on his back. After that he didn't move.

The first man got up on one knee and took aim at me again. I shifted the Spencer, levering in a third shell. The man fired at almost the same instant that I did.

His bullet felt like a hot iron in the muscles of my upper arm. But my bullet caught him squarely between the eyes, driving him back the way the other man had been. Neither of them moved again.

I stood there in a kind of numb bewilderment. Everything had happened so fast it was still hard for me to believe. Charlie Two Horses lay spread-eagled in the street with the rope end still around his neck. The two men lay sprawled awkwardly not far away.

There was noise in the street suddenly, the sounds of many voices, of running feet. I turned and looked at all the people coming down the street and out of the stores. I wondered where they'd been a few minutes ago when I'd needed help.

They stared at the bodies in the street with white faces, with shock and unbelieving eyes. I wanted to run and hide. They turned to stare at me as if I was a stranger and not someone who belonged right here in Twin Forks.

I stared back, having the strange feeling that I didn't really belong there at all. Suddenly I dropped the gun and ran. I ran up Main Street until I reached Elm, the street our house was on. I turned into Elm and ran until I came home.

I stumbled up the walk and across the porch. I slammed into the house, ran to my room and threw myself full length on the bed.

I felt grandpa's presence and looked around. He was standing in the door. He asked, "What's the matter, Jesse?"

He must have seen the blood on my shoulder then because he crossed the room and sat down beside me on the bed. His eyes were stern now, and filled with anger. "What happened? What happened to you?"

I knew if I said anything I was going to cry. I began to shake.

Grandpa said sharply, "Jesse! Stop that and talk!" There was no longer any gentleness in his voice.

I clenched my fists. I said, "Two men roped Charlie Two Horses and dragged him. I cut him loose and they dragged me. When I got loose I got a gun. . . ." My teeth were chattering so badly that I couldn't go on.

But he wouldn't let me stop. "Damn it, tell me what happened."

"I killed them."

"You what?"

"I killed them."

His bony face was stern, the skin brown and stretched tight over it. His eyes were narrowed and very blue. His mouth was a thin, straight line. Grandpa was seventy-five though he didn't look that old.

"For God's sake why? Why did you kill them? For dragging you?"

"Because they killed Charlie Two Horses. And because they'd have killed me too if I hadn't killed them first."

He stared down at me. What he was feeling was all mixed up in his face. At last he said helplessly, "Damn it, Jesse, we have a sheriff to handle things like that!"

I stared back at him defiantly. "Then where was he? Where was he when Charlie Two Horses was getting killed? Where was he when I was getting dragged?"

"He can't be everywhere."

My shoulder was paining me something fierce. I felt sick to my stomach. I guess he saw how green I was getting because he told me to lie down. I did and closed my eyes and he cut my shirt away from my shoulder wound.

Almost as if I was dreaming, I heard him talking to himself: "Bullet went clean through. Missed the bone."

His hands were gentle but I fainted in spite of my determination not to. When I came to I was under the covers, the dirt washed off me, and I was wearing my nightshirt instead of my ragged clothes. My shoulder had a bulky bandage over it.

II

THE WAY the sun was shining in my window told me it was afternoon. I could hear voices downstairs, my grandpa's voice and someone else's too. After a while I heard footsteps on the stairs and grandpa came to the door. "How do you feel?"

"All right, I guess." I didn't, though. I felt terrible. My head ached something awful and I felt like I was going to be sick. My shoulder and arm were just one big throbbing pain.

He said, "The sheriff's here. He wants to talk to you."

"All right."

He went into the hall and called downstairs. "You can come up now, Burt."

I heard Sheriff Coffey's footsteps on the stairs. A moment later he came into the room.

He was a solid man, not as tall as I but broad and strong. He wore a sweeping, tawny mustache about the color of prairie grass in August when it's dry. His face was serious. He held his broad-brimmed hat in his hands "I want your story of what happened, Jesse." He looked at grandpa. "It's all right if I question him, isn't it, Mr. Hand?"

Grandpa said sourly, "Since when am I Mr. Hand? Hell yes, it's all right. Go ahead."

I said, "One of them kicked Charlie Two Horses when he came out of the saloon. They got on their horses and started to ride away but one of them changed his mind and came back. He roped Charlie and dragged him down the street. When he turned around and came back, I ran out and cut the rope."

"Then what?"

"I looked at Charlie and saw that he was dead. Before I could do anything, they roped me and dragged me the way they'd just dragged him. I still had my knife and I managed to cut the rope. They were coming for me but I ran between them and got a rifle off one of their horses."

"Who shot first, Jesse? You or them?"

"I guess I did."

Grandpa said, "You're nit-picking, Burt. It was self-defense, even if he did fire first. They had already killed Charlie Two Horses. They had dragged Jesse. He was justified in thinking they'd kill him unless he defended himself."

Burt Coffey stared at grandpa. "You telling me how to do my job?"

"Maybe."

Coffey's face got red. He glared at grandpa and grandpa glared right back. At last the sheriff said sourly, "The people in town are thinking about his pa."

"What the hell has his pa got to do with this?"

Coffey shrugged. "They're saying, 'Like father, like son.'"

Grandpa said a word that I'd have been walloped

for using. He looked at the sheriff disgustedly. "That's a lot of hogwash and you know it. Jesse tried to protect Charlie Two Horses from an unprovoked attack. That's all there is to it."

Coffey shrugged again. "Maybe. Maybe not. There'll be a coroner's inquest anyway. The coroner's jury will decide what's to be done."

"What's to be done? Why Jesus Christ . . . !"

"Cussin' ain't going to change anything. There's been two killin's and somebody's got to pay for 'em."

Grandpa said furiously, "Three killings, Burt. Or don't you count Indians?"

Sheriff Coffey's face got red again.

Grandpa's tone still was furious. "You've asked your questions, Burt. You can find your own way out."

Coffey grunted something that I didn't understand. He turned and went out. I heard him clumping down the stairs and I heard the front door slam.

Grandpa went to the window and stared outside. I asked, "What did he mean about my pa?"

He was silent for a long time. I was about to repeat the question when he turned and looked at me. He said, "I guess it's time you knew. It's bound to come out anyway and I'd a heap rather you heard it from me."

He sat down in a chair. He gripped his knees with his hands so tightly that the knuckles turned white.

16

He said, "You were only two years old when your pa was killed."

"Killed? How?"

"By a sheriff's posse. He wouldn't surrender and they shot him down."

"What had he done? Why were they after him?"

His face looked like he was in pain. He said, "Your pa got the idea that your ma wasn't true to him. It wasn't so, but he believed it and killed the man he thought had been seeing her." His voice took on a note of angry bitterness. "It doesn't matter now, I guess, but I always figured they wouldn't have shot him down if the man he killed hadn't been so prominent in the Free State movement."

I didn't remember my mother at all but I had seen an old tintype of her once. I asked, "What happened to her?"

He turned his head and stared at me. "That's the hell of it, Jesse. I don't know. She couldn't stay here after it happened. People kept saying that where there was smoke there had to be fire. So she left. She said she'd write but she never did. She just disappeared."

The shock of hearing how my father had died had been bad enough. The shock of being told that my mother had just disappeared was worse. I wanted to ask how she could have left me without even trying to see me again, but I couldn't. So I didn't say anything.

Grandpa said, "Jesse, something must have happened to her. She was going to write as soon as she got located and I was going to take you to her. I tried to find out what had happened but I never could. She went to St. Louis and she just plain disappeared. She didn't get in touch with your Aunt Carrie like I thought she would."

I wanted grandpa to go. I didn't want to hear any more. I just wanted to be alone. At last I heard the chair creak and his footsteps went to the door. The door closed quietly and I heard him going down the stairs.

I didn't open my eyes and I didn't unclench my fists. I was thinking about my father, shot to death by a posse. I was thinking of my mother, driven out of town because people believed the worst of her. Something terrible must have happened to her. Otherwise she'd have written or come back.

I'd thought the townspeople had looked at me kind of funny downtown a while ago. They had probably looked at her the same way after the posse shot my father down. As if they had already made up their minds about her. They probably hadn't tried to help her any more than they'd tried to help me a while ago.

About me they were saying, "Like father, like son." They'd sit on that coroner's jury and they'd probably say I had to go to trial. I'd go to prison and rot there and nobody would even care.

I was feeling pretty sorry for myself when I fell

asleep. It was dark when I woke up. I got up and went downstairs, holding onto the banister so I wouldn't fall. I was pretty light-headed and dizzy and I was mighty weak.

Grandpa was in the kitchen. He made me sit down and he brought me some bread and cold meat and milk. Eating made me feel a little better and I went back upstairs and crawled into bed again. When I woke a second time it was light outside.

I got up and dressed. My shoulder was awfully sore and I still felt weak, but I didn't want to lay around anymore. I had a job down at Blumenthal's that I didn't want to lose. Besides, I wanted to see Julia. I wanted to know if she felt the way the rest of the people in town seemed to feel about what I'd done.

I don't mind admitting that I was getting mad. I figured I'd done what was right, what the sheriff would have done if he'd been around. I figured it was pretty raw to be blamed for doing right. On top of that, I was mad about my pa being shot to death by some of these same townspeople and I was mad about ma being forced to leave because of their wagging tongues. I figured if she was dead it was them that were to blame.

I went downstairs. I was still dizzy but I was a lot better than I'd been the day before. Grandpa was gone so I got myself some milk and scrambled some eggs on the stove. Afterward I shaved and combed my hair. I hadn't been able to get the shirt on over the bandage and my arm felt awkward inside the shirt. I went out and walked downtown to Blumenthal's.

By the time I got there lights were flashing in front of my eyes. I was sweating and afraid I was going to faint right there on the street. I managed to get inside Blumenthal's and the cool air made me feel better than I had before.

Mr. Blumenthal came waddling up to the front end of the store. He was clucking at me sympathetically, but there was something funny about the way he kept looking at the floor. I said, "I'm sorry I couldn't get to work this morning, Mr. Blumenthal. But I guess you know what happened yesterday."

He nodded, still clucking. "I know. I know. A terrible, terrible thing."

I said, "I can probably come back to work in about a week."

He looked embarrassed and he still wouldn't look at me. "I was meaning to tell you before all this happened, Jesse. I don't need you anymore. It's a slack time of year and I can do the work myself."

I said, "It's funny you didn't tell me before the shooting. It makes me wonder if you're not letting me go because of that."

He turned, not even bothering to deny that it was true. "Come back to the office, Jesse, and I'll give you your pay."

I followed him back to the office and he paid me in gold, fifty cents a day for twenty days. He gave me two five-dollar gold pieces. I walked back to the front of the store. Two women had come in and it was pretty plain that they were talking about me. Neither spoke to me although I knew both of them pretty well.

I kept getting madder and madder as I walked up the street. I was sick to my stomach and weak and dizzy and my shoulder hurt like hell. I headed for the Delisa house at the upper end of town. The way I was feeling I wasn't even sure I'd get that far. I wondered what would happen if I just fell down and died. I remember thinking that they'd all be sorry then. They'd be sorry for the way they'd treated me when they found me lying dead.

But I didn't fall down. I kept on toward the Delisa house. Julia must have seen me coming up the street because she came running to meet me. She pulled me off the walk and over behind a clump of lilac bushes that were in full bloom. I still can't smell lilacs without remembering that day just as clearly as if it was yesterday.

Julia was about a head shorter than me. She had smooth brown hair and skin that was real white and soft. Her eyes were blue and they had tears in them. "Jesse, you're hurt!"

"It ain't nothing."

"I'd have come to see you yesterday when I heard, but—"

"But what?"

"Nothing. Does it hurt very bad?"

"It ain't nothing. It hurts but not so bad I can't stand it."

"I'm so proud of you."

"Then you're about the only one who is. Old man Blumenthal just fired me."

"For what you did?"

I shrugged. "What else?" I remembered what she'd said about wanting to come to see me so I asked, "Why didn't you come to see me when you heard that I'd been shot?"

"I . . . pa wouldn't let me come. He said—" She stopped.

"What did he say?"

"Jesse, it doesn't matter. It doesn't matter at all."

"It matters to me. What did he say?"

She stood on tiptoe. "Jesse, kiss me."

"What did he say?"

Tears filled her eyes and spilled over to run across her cheeks. I felt like a dog but I had to know what her pa had said. I insisted, "Julia, I've got to know."

Her face flushed a little. She wiped the tears away and when she looked at me there was anger where the tears had been. "He said you were like your pa. He said you'd come to a bad end just like he did. He said I wasn't to see you anymore, no matter what. He said if I did he'd wallop me and wallop you."

I don't know what I'd have said. I didn't have a chance to say anything I heard someone coming and turned my head.

It was Julia's pa. He grabbed me by the arm and yanked me away from her. It wasn't my hurt arm, but getting yanked like that hurt so bad that for a minute I could hardly stand. I guess I staggered against him and maybe he thought I'd tried to hit him or something. Anyway he hit me with his fist right on the nose.

I sat down, my nose streaming blood. Julia's mother had come up behind her father, and now she was screaming at me. Julia was crying and they began yelling at her too. Her father grabbed her by the arm and dragged her back up the street toward their house. Her mother followed, after screeching something at me that I didn't understand.

I began to cuss the lousy people in this town, for what they'd done to my father and to my mother and for what they were doing now to me. It was like they were trying to make me end up like my father had. It was like they wanted to see me shot down like he had been.

III

I DIDN'T stay there on the grass for very long. I was too mad. I got up and slouched away toward home, thinking of all the things I'd like to do to Julia's pa. I ought to do him like I'd done the two strangers down on Main Street yesterday. Damn him anyway.

I was seventeen years old and it sure was beginning to look like I couldn't stay in Twin Forks anymore. I began to think about going away. I could go hunt gold in Colorado, I thought. I'd stay long enough to strike it rich and then I'd come back here driving a fancy carriage with two high-stepping, gleaming bays up front. I'd drive down the street and I wouldn't even look at any of the people standing on the walk watching me. I'd drive right up to the Delisa house and Julia would come out and I'd help her up into the carriage and drive away with her.

I figured I could make it, going away, even though the thought of it scared the hell out of me. I had a little money put away from working at Blumenthal's. Forty-seven dollars to be exact. And I had the two five-dollar gold pieces Blumenthal had given me when he fired me.

Grandpa met me at the door. His eyes were worried. "You ought to be in bed. You've got to give that shoulder time to heal."

I said, "Blumenthal fired me. And Julia's pa said I wasn't to see her anymore."

"There are other jobs. And Julia's pa will get over it."

"I don't think so. Anyhow, I'm going away."

He didn't say anything for quite a while. He just kept looking at me as if he was trying to see inside my mind.

At last he said, "You're sure that's what you want?"

"It's what I want." But I wasn't too sure it was.

"Where will you go? Back to your Aunt Carrie's in St. Louis?"

I shook my head. "Out west, I suppose. Over to Colorado, to hunt gold, maybe." I'd lived with Aunt Carrie until about a year ago. I didn't want to go back there.

"When you going?"

"As soon as I can. As soon as the inquest is over with. You reckon they'll put me in jail?"

He shook his head. "I wouldn't worry about that."

I knew if I waited very long I wouldn't go at all. I was still scared of going but I was beginning to feel excited too. Waiting for the inquest would give my shoulder time to heal. By the time it was over with, the shoulder ought to be in pretty good shape again.

Grandpa said, "You can take old Duke. And you can take my saddle. I don't use it much any more."

I nodded. I went past him and into the house and climbed the stairs to my room. I laid down and stared at the ceiling for a long time before I finally went to sleep.

The inquest was held a week after the shooting. Grandpa went to the courthouse with me. I saw Mr. Blumenthal there, and Mr. and Mrs. Delisa, but not Julia.

The county coroner had me tell my story. Then he asked questions of some of the witnesses. Mr. Blumenthal was one of the witnesses. Mr. Blumenthal was one of the ones who had watched that day but who hadn't done anything. I kept wondering if anyone was going to ask him and the others why they hadn't interfered, but nobody did. I guess they were trying to spare the witnesses' feelings but nobody seemed worried about sparing mine. I felt like everybody was staring accusingly at me all the time I was there.

Finally the coroner gave his verdict: "Justifiable homicide committed by Jesse Hand in the defense of his life."

We got up and left the courtroom. It seemed to me like some of the people looked disappointed.

I didn't like the people of Twin Forks very much that day. I blamed them for my father's death and for the fact that my mother had gone away. I blamed them for not helping me in the street the day the two strangers dragged Charlie Two Horses to death. Plenty of them had seen what was happening but none had interfered. I realize now that they were ashamed of not helping me, but I didn't know it then.

Grandpa didn't say much to me when we got home, but several times that evening I caught him watching me. I knew he wanted me to stay. I could see it in his eyes. But the thought of leaving had gotten hold of me by then and I knew I had to go.

Next morning I went out and saddled up old Duke. Grandpa gave me a pair of saddlebags that he had filled with food and extra clothes. He tied a roll of blankets behind the saddle.

I got up on Duke's back. Grandpa stuck up his hand to me. "Write now, Jesse. Your home's here anytime you want to come back to it."

I shook his hand. I tried to grin at him as I said, "Goodbye grandpa." I turned Duke and rode away. I looked back as I went around the corner. Grandpa was still standing there watching me, holding up a hand to shade his eyes from the glare of the rising sun. I waved and he waved back and then I couldn't see him anymore.

I rode out of town, wanting to go by the Delisa house but not doing it. A dirt road headed west and I followed it.

About ten miles from town I came to a stream and I let Duke drink and got down to drink myself. I went on and stopped again maybe twenty miles from town when the sun was directly overhead.

I ate some meat and bread from the saddlebags. I was sitting there finishing up when I heard a horse coming along the road.

Pretty soon the horse came around a bend. A man was riding him. He didn't belong in Twin Forks but I'd seen him at the inquest the day before.

He was around fifty, I suppose, because his hair and whiskers were gray. He was fat around the middle but his arms were muscular and he had a thick neck and a balding head that looked too big for him. He saw me and grinned and came straight toward me. "Well looky here," he said. "It's Jesse Hand, the kid who shot the two drifters back in town."

For some reason he made me feel uneasy and I didn't want him around. I said, "I'm leaving. I just stopped to eat."

"Come on, now," he said, "don't be so unsociable. Ain't you even going to offer old Dan McGinnis a bite?"

I said, "I ain't got more'n enough to take me to the next town."

He looked hurt, but he wasn't really hurt, just putting on. I got up and headed for my horse.

McGinnis was off his horse real quick and when he hit the ground he was right between me and Duke. He was still grinning that oily grin but his eyes were cold as ice. I tried to get past him but he caught my sleeve and when I tried to pull away he hit me with his fist. It felt like a mule had kicked me in the jaw and the next thing I knew I was flat on my back on the ground.

I sat up. "What the hell's the matter with you? What'd you do that for anyway?"

"What you got in your pockets, Jesse? Anything Old Dan can use?"

I understood. He was going to rob me. He didn't figure I'd go back to Twin Forks to complain, and even if I did he'd be fifty miles from here by the time the sheriff could get back with me.

There were only two things for it, run or fight and running sure didn't appeal much to me. I looked around for something to fight him with but there wasn't a thing. Not a rock, not a stick, not anything.

He stood there spraddle-legged, grinning that nasty grin at me. "What's it to be, Jesse, empty your pockets or fight?"

"I ain't going to empty my pockets."

The answer seemed to please him. He nodded. "All right, Jesse. We'll do it the hard way then," and he started toward me.

I got up. When he was close enough, I made a run for him. Any kid my age has been in a fistfight or two. I swung a haymaker at him that connected solidly with the side of his head. Trouble was, it didn't affect him at all. He grabbed me with both hands. I kept trying to hit him but I knew if that first solid blow hadn't affected him, nothing I could do to him would. He let loose of me with his right hand and hit me in the mouth. Then he hit me in the nose. I could taste blood and the pain in my nose made tears fill my eyes so I could hardly see.

He began to chuckle as though he enjoyed what he was doing to me. He kept hitting me, over and over again in the mouth and nose and eyes while he held me up with his other hand. Things were whirling. My mouth felt puffy and my nose felt like it was too big for my face. My eyes felt like they were swelled up and nearly closed. At last he let me go and I fell on the ground. I groaned and moved a little, I guess, because he kicked me in the side, not once but several times. He said in that same nasty, wheedling voice, "Now, Jesse, let's see what you've got in your pockets for old Dan."

I tried to roll and get away from him but no matter how I tried, I couldn't move. I felt him going through my pockets. He found the fifty-seven dollars in gold and the silver watch that had belonged to my pa. I heard him walk away. I heard him mount his horse and I heard the sound of hoofs. I was hanging onto consciousness but it didn't do any good. Things went black and suddenly I didn't know any more.

When I woke up it was dark. I hurt all over. My shoulder wound had opened up while he was beating me and now my shirt was stuck to it and it hurt like hell. My face was one big puffy mass of pain. Both my eyes were completely closed so that I couldn't see. My nose was swelled up and so was my mouth. I tried to lick my lips but they were stuck together with dried blood.

I could hear the sound of running water and the breeze in the trees, but nothing else. And it was cold. I guess the cold had wakened me.

I was terribly thirsty so I crawled toward the sound of water. I probably had broken ribs, I thought, where he had kicked me. I might die out here but if I didn't, I made myself a promise that some day I was going to find Dan McGinnis and pay him back.

I reached the stream bank and, feeling ahead for water with my hands, found it. I buried my face in the cold water and began to wash off the blood with my hands. This way, I finally got my mouth open enough to take a drink and ran my tongue over my lips again. I found out my eyes weren't swelled clear shut. The lids had been stuck together with blood just as my mouth had been. I could open them just a slit and I could see, though not very well.

He should have killed me when he had the chance, I thought. Because I was going to find him and I was going to kill him if it was the last thing I ever did.

He could never have done this to me at all if I'd had a gun. Back in Twin Forks, the two strangers could never have dragged me, either, if I'd had a gun. I made myself a promise that I was going to get me a gun as soon as I could, and learn to use it, and never be without it as long as I lived. Nobody was ever going to beat me again, or drag me again at the end of a rope.

I began to look around for Duke. He'd not have gone far, I thought. But I guess I knew all the time that I wasn't going to find him. He was gone along with my money and my watch, along with grandpa's saddle and my blankets and food.

IV

I KNEW I had a choice. I could walk the twenty miles back to Twin Forks or I could go on. If I went back to Twin Forks I'd probably stay there the rest of my life. Maybe in time I could live down both what I'd done and what my father had done but I'd be like a whipped pup, crawling back with my tail between my legs. Dan McGinnis would get away with what he'd done to me because it was a cinch the sheriff would never catch up with him. It was doubtful he'd even try.

I was hurting all over and I was colder than I'd ever been in my life before. The thought of my bed at home and of grandpa to take care of me was tempting, I have to admit.

The sun came up finally and it wasn't long before I began to get warm again. I got up and hobbled down the road, still heading west. I wanted Dan McGinnis. But mostly, I guess, I wanted to prove something to myself. I was hurt but I was a long ways from being a whipped pup with my tail between my legs.

Kansas is mighty big. It stretches away in rolling hills for several hundred miles and you don't travel it very fast on foot. I was scared because I had no money and no food. I knew I didn't have a chance of staying on Dan McGinnis's trail. I had to stop and work until I had enough money to go on. I had to face the fact that for the time being at least, Dan McGinnis would get away with what he'd done to me.

I walked all that day without seeing anyone. At last, near sundown, I saw a farmhouse ahead. I didn't think I could walk as far as the house but I kept putting one foot ahead of the other, keeping my eyes on the house. I reached it just as it was getting dark. A couple of dogs ran out and barked at me. A man came out of the barn and peered at me through the last gray light of dusk. I shuffled toward him and when I reached him sat down numbly on the ground. I said, "I'm Jesse Hand. I was beaten and robbed yesterday."

The man was bearded. He looked stern. He studied me for a long time. "What do you want from me?"

I said, "I'm sure hungry and I could use a place to sleep. But I don't want nothing unless I work for it."

He nodded. He went back into the barn and I could hear milk squirting into a bucket as he finished milking his cow. The dogs sniffed at me but they didn't bark. After a while the man came out with a bucket in his hand. He said, "All right, come on up to the house. You can wash over there at the pump."

I went over to the pump and washed the best I could. I went on to the house and he came to the door and let me in. There were two women inside, an old one and a younger one that must have been his wife. I sat down where he told me to and ate like I hadn't eaten for a month. When I'd finished, he said, "You can sleep in the hayloft. You ain't got no matches, have you?"

I shook my head. He said, "You can work here for your keep, just so's you work."

I said, "I got to get some money too. I got to go on west."

"We ain't got money here. Keep's all you'll get. If you don't like that, you can move along."

I went out to the barn and climbed up to the loft. I was sure hurting and I was so discouraged I wanted to just up and quit. How was I going to go on if I couldn't get any money for a gun or for a horse? How was I going to catch Dan McGinnis?

I laid down in the hay and closed my eyes. I began to get mad as I lay there thinking about it. I didn't know how I was going to go on but I was. I finally went to sleep.

It seemed like I'd hardly shut my eyes before I heard the farmer yelling down below. I got up and climbed down the ladder. It was still dark outside. He told me to go out after the cow, so I did. I drove her in and milked her and carried the milk to the house. I ate breakfast and as soon as it was over with, he led me out to the barn again and we hitched up a team. He drove the team out to one of his fields and hooked the horse to a plow. He showed me how to loop the reins around my neck and how to guide the plow. By the time the sun came up, I was walking around the field behind the plow.

My shoulder wound opened up and began to bleed. My ribs, where McGinnis had kicked me, hurt every time the plowhandles jerked. My face was just one solid mass of pain.

I'd been plowing several hours and was about ready to lie down and die when a man on a horse turned in and rode down the lane. He saw me in the field and rode his horse out to where I was. I said, "Whoa," at the team and leaned on the plow to rest.

He stared at my face. "What happened to you?"

"What's it look like? I got beat up."

"By who? Where?"

"By a guy that called himself Dan McGinnis. Back down the road a ways."

He looked at me closer than he had before. "You wouldn't be Jesse Hand, would you?"

"What if I am?"

"Nothing. Except I heard about you back in Twin Forks. They said you were heading west."

"I was until he took my horse."

"You working here trying to earn another one?"

"I'm working here so's I can eat."

"I'm heading west. How'd you like to go with me?"

I looked at him suspiciously. He said, "I heard

what you did back there in Twin Forks a couple of weeks ago. I guess I like your spunk. But don't feel like you have to go."

I stared up at him. He was a medium-sized man, not heavily built like Dan McGinnis had been. He had steady gray eyes and a mustache like Sheriff Coffey in Twin Forks. He wore a broad-brimmed hat like the hats the two strangers that killed Charlie Two Horses had worn. His right hand was shrunken and twisted almost like a claw.

I said, "Wait until I unhitch this team and drive 'em back to the barn."

I did, and the stranger followed me. I didn't know why he'd offered to let me go with him and I didn't care. All I could think was that now I'd have a chance of catching up with McGinnis. He'd know I was hurt and he'd know I was afoot. He wouldn't be worried about me catching up with him, so maybe he wouldn't be hurrying.

The farmer grumbled when I told him I was leaving but I figured I'd plowed enough to pay him for the two meals he'd given me and for the use of his loft. I climbed up on the stranger's horse behind him and we headed west. As soon as we were on the road he half-turned around and stuck out his crippled hand. "I'm Ben Hackett, Jesse."

I took the hand and shook it. I wondered what had happened to it but I didn't ask.

We rode pretty steady all that day. Hackett didn't push his horse. He kept him at a plodding walk all the time. When night came, we still hadn't come to any towns. We'd passed about two farmhouses but that was all.

We stopped on the bank of a little stream. While Hackett unsaddled and picketed his horse in the long grass, I gathered wood for a fire. I shaved a stick until I had a pile of shavings. Then I added little twigs and lastly I put on the bigger sticks. Hackett gave me a match and I lighted it.

He had some blackened pots tied behind his saddle, along with a guitar in a sack and a blanket roll. He also had a gunny sack with some grub in it. He mixed up some batter and made flapjacks, fried some salt pork to go with them and then made coffee. He only had one plate and one cup, so he let me eat first.

While I was eating, and it was a slow and painful process, he took the guitar out of the sack and sat down by the fire with it. He strummed a few chords and then, surprisingly, began to sing. His voice was nasal, but pleasant enough to hear.

Billy Venero heard them say, in an Arizona town one day, That a band of Apache Indians were upon the trail of death, Heard them tell of murder done, three men killed in Rocky Run They're in danger at the Cow Ranch, *said Venero under his breath. Cow Ranch, forty miles away, was a little place that lay In a deep and shady valley in the mighty wilderness. Half a score of homes were there and in one a maiden fair Held the heart of Billy Venero, Billy Venero's little Bess.*

The song had a lot of verses. In the end Billy Venero rode his horse down the little lane at the Cow Ranch and died in Bess's arms of wounds inflicted by the Indians. I'd finished eating by then, so Ben Hackett ate. Afterwards he washed the dishes and pots with sand at the stream and put them away. He said, "I know you want to catch McGinnis. We'll sleep an hour or so and then go on."

That plodding walk he'd maintained all day had fooled me. I hadn't figured he was going to hurry any trying to catch McGinnis for me. Now it looked like he'd planned on catching McGinnis all along.

I laid down beside the fire and closed my eyes. He laid down on the other side of it. I began to think about what it would be like coming face to face with McGinnis if we were lucky enough to catch up with him.

I knew I'd have to have a gun. I hadn't been able to stand up to him with my fists before and I'd have no better chance now. But if I had a gun. . . . I said, "You got a gun, Mr. Hackett?"

"Six-shooter. In my saddlebag."

"You reckon I could use it if we catch up with McGinnis?"

"Ever shoot one, Jesse?"

"Nope. But if I can shoot a rifle I can shoot a six-shooter."

"You can use it, Jesse. I'll show you how tomorrow."

I said, "Thanks, Mr. Hackett." I had the funny feeling that he'd intended on letting me use the gun even before I asked. I didn't understand Ben Hackett but maybe it wasn't necessary that I understand. It was enough that he was taking me along with him, that he was helping me catch McGinnis. I owed him a mighty lot for that.

I went sound asleep right away but it seemed like only a few minutes before I heard Ben Hackett saying, "Come on, Jesse. Get up. It's time we were on our way."

I got up. He had the horse saddled and ready to go. He'd killed the fire. It was dark but there was a crescent moon in the sky that gave off a little light. I climbed up behind him and we rode away, heading west.

We rode at that same steady walk all night. It got steadily colder and I ached worse than I ever had in my life before.

I was glad to see the eastern sky turn gray and I was a lot gladder to see the sun come up. When the sun was well above the horizon Ben Hackett stopped his horse. He threw a leg over the horse's neck and slid to the ground. He knelt in the dusty road and studied the ground for several minutes, then turned his head and looked up at me. "Tracks. Two horses. Could be McGinnis."

I said, "My horse had a split in his right front hoof."

He studied the ground some more, finally standing up. "It's McGinnis, Jesse. And the tracks were made last night."

I asked, "Any towns ahead?"

"Yep. About ten miles. Town called Cherokee."

He mounted and we went on, still moving at a steady walk. I was thinking that if the tracks had been made last night, then McGinnis had probably gone on into Cherokee before he stopped for the night. It would have been pretty late by the time he arrived so he probably wouldn't be leaving very early today. We might catch him in Cherokee or we might catch him just west of it.

I wanted to tell Hackett to hurry but I didn't. He'd gotten me this close to McGinnis I had a feeling he'd do a lot better than that before the day was out. I figured we were going to catch McGinnis today.

V

AFTER A while we passed a sign that said Cherokee was five miles away. Hackett reined his horse off to one side of the road and into a little grove of trees. He slid off and I followed suit. He rummaged in one of his cracked leather saddlebags and finally brought out the gun.

It was an old Army Colt revolver. It had originally been a percussion gun but it had been converted to take .44 caliber cartridges. He handed it to me, studying my face. "If we're going to catch up with McGinnis, you'd better be ready for him."

I raised the gun and sighted a rock with it. He said, "Thumb the hammer back all the way. Then see if you can hit that rock."

I thumbed the hammer back. The gun was heavy but it felt good in my hand. I sighted, held my breath and pulled the trigger. A puff of dust came from the rock and the bullet whined away.

I looked at Ben Hackett. He said, "I wondered how you were able to kill those two back in Twin Forks so easily. Now I guess I know. See if you can hit the rock again."

I thumbed the hammer back and fired at the rock again. Again dust puffed from it and the bullet whined away. Hackett said, "Try it without sighting. Like you were pointing your finger at what you meant to hit."

I lowered the gun and stared at the rock. I made believe I was pointing my finger at the rock instead of pointing the gun at it. I thumbed back the hammer and fired again. The bullet missed by six inches or so. I glanced at Hackett.

His eyes had a funny glow to them. He breathed, "You're the one, Jesse. You're the one!"

"What do you mean, I'm the one? I missed it clean."

"Yeah, but this is the first time you've ever had a

pistol in your hand. You'll do, Jesse. Let's go catch McGinnis now. Just keep the pistol stuffed down in your belt."

He took it from me and reloaded it, then gave it back to me. I got up on the horse behind him, the gun stuck down in my belt.

He headed toward Cherokee, trotting the horse for the first time. I bounced up and down and the motion made my ribs and shoulder hurt but I didn't care. If the horse trotted it meant we'd catch McGinnis that much sooner.

Being anxious didn't make the distance any less, but eventually we came to the town of Cherokee. It squatted along the bank of a stream with high bluffs on the north side and a wide flat on the south. It was a smaller town than Twin Forks. It had four buildings on one side of the main street and six on the other. Besides these ten buildings there were probably half a dozen houses. Shacks was more like it, I figured.

Hackett stopped his horse in front of the hotel. He slid off and right away got his rifle out of the saddle boot. I got down and adjusted the six-shooter in my belt so it wouldn't catch when I tried to get it out.

There were a couple of old men on the hotel porch. Hackett asked, "Did a man named McGinnis stay here last night?"

One of the old men shrugged. The other asked, "What'd he look like?"

Hackett glanced at me. I said, "Bald. Big belly. Maybe around fifty years old."

Both men nodded. "He stayed here."

"Is he still here?"

"Ain't come out less'n he came out afore we got up."

Hackett said, "Stay here, Jesse. I'll go inside and see."

He went into the hotel. I wanted to take the six-shooter out of my belt so I'd be ready for McGinnis but I didn't. I glued my eyes to the door and didn't look away.

I suppose I'd waited five minutes before the door banged open and Dan McGinnis came out. I said, "Didn't expect to see me, did you?"

He looked startled. Then he began to grin. He was picking his teeth and grinning as he came toward me. I said, "I'm going to turn you over to the law. Turn around and put your hands up behind your head."

He kept grinning and coming toward me. The same look was on his face that had been there just before he started beating me back on the road. I put my hand on the gun. I said, "You stop or I'm going to kill you."

He stopped. He rolled the toothpick back and forth in his mouth. I watched it, for a moment forgetting to watch his hands.

A yell from the hotel doorway woke me up. It was Hackett and he yelled, "Jesse! He's got a gun!"

Sure enough, McGinnis's hand was coming out of his back pocket and there was a little double-barreled derringer in it. I grabbed for the gun in my belt. The front sight caught and for a minute I was sure I was going to be killed. The derringer kept coming up. . . .

Behind McGinnis, Hackett came slamming out of the hotel. He bawled, "McGinnis! Behind you!"

McGinnis didn't turn. But he hesitated the barest fraction of a second.

It was enough. My gun cleared and I thumbed the hammer back as it did. I kept it coming up to eye level, sighting on McGinnis's chest. I fired and saw a look of surprise come into his eyes.

His derringer fired and the bullet tore into the ground at my feet, kicking up a puff of dust.

McGinnis staggered back and slammed into the wall of the hotel. He slid down the wall to a sitting position. I'd thought there was going to be a lot of satisfaction in this for me but there wasn't. There wasn't any satisfaction at all. McGinnis's head sagged forward and lolled to one side and I knew that he was dead.

Hackett stood over McGinnis, looking down. He asked, "How much did he take from you, Jesse?"

"Fifty-seven dollars in gold. And my horse."

Hackett knelt and started going through McGinnis's pockets. A voice behind me said, "Hold it, mister. Hold it right there. You think you can kill a man and rob him right here on the street in broad daylight?"

I turned my head. A scrawny middle-aged man with a star on his vest and a gravy stain on his shirt-front was standing at the foot of the steps leading up to the hotel porch. I said, "He robbed me. He took fifty-seven dollars in gold from me and my horse and saddle. Besides that, he beat me up."

The scrawny man shrugged. "Mebbe. Mebbe not. It ain't for me to decide. All I got to worry about is holding you in jail until the circuit judge gets here. I'll see that the dead man gets buried and I'll hold whatever he's got until the judge says what to do with it."

Hackett had gotten up. His rifle was in his hands. It was pointing straight at the deputy. Hackett said, "Finish going through his pockets, Jesse."

I stared at him. He said, "Jesse, that circuit judge might not come through here for weeks. I don't know about you but I'm not going to lay in jail that long. Not for McGinnis. Not for this rooster with the badge, either."

I looked at the deputy. I said, "I told him I was going to turn him over to the law but he went for his gun. He didn't give me any choice."

Hackett said, "Get your money, Jesse, and don't argue with him."

I persisted, "How about it, mister? I ought to have a right to get back what he took from me."

He said, "You'll get it when the judge says so. Put down your gun, boy, and don't listen to him. He'll make an outlaw out of you if you do."

I looked at Hackett and back at the deputy. I didn't have much confidence in the law and I suppose that was what decided me. I finished going through McGinnis's pockets and came up with his money pouch and pa's silver watch. I opened the pouch and poured the coins into my other hand. I took fifty-seven dollars in gold and put it in my pocket. The rest I put back in the pouch. I tightened the drawstrings and tossed it to the deputy.

Hackett said, "Come on, deputy. You can walk to the livery barn with us."

The deputy didn't say anything. He walked ahead of us down the street to the livery barn. We went in and while Hackett kept his rifle on the deputy, I located my horse and saddle. I threw the saddle on, cinched it down and led the horse to where Hackett and the deputy were.

Hackett got on his horse and I got on mine. Hackett said, "Don't come after us, deputy."

The deputy just looked at him. He wasn't afraid but he seemed to know there was no use arguing.

There was a little crowd out in front of the hotel as we rode out, heading west. Hackett grinned at me. "Feel better, Jesse, now that you've got your horse and money back?"

I nodded, but I doubt if I convinced Hackett and I sure didn't convince myself. I had a strange, upsetting feeling, like I was a train on a track. It was like I had no control over where I was going. I felt helpless but I didn't know what to do about it.

Hackett had helped me and I owed him something. Without his help I'd still be stuck back at that farm, working for my grub. Besides, neither one of us had really done anything wrong. I hadn't wanted to kill McGinnis. He hadn't given me a choice.

Hackett trotted on ahead and I let Duke lag back twenty or thirty yards. I was asking myself some searching questions and I didn't like the answers I gave myself. Had I really been as innocent of wrongdoing as I thought? I'd hated McGinnis for beating me. I'd had the gun all ready and maybe I hadn't given him any more choice than he'd given me. I'd forced him to draw and then had shot him down. Hackett's interference, his sudden shout, had only made it possible.

I stared gloomily at Hackett's back. He had helped me and I owed him for that, but was he helping me now or was he using me?

I touched my heels to Duke's sides and ranged up beside him in the road. I asked, "You reckon that deputy will be coming after us?"

"Maybe. Depends on whether he can get up a posse."

"And what if he can't get up a posse?"

"What do you mean?"

"Will he post us as fugitives?"

Hackett looked at me irritably. "Hell, Jesse, how would I know what that deputy is going to do? If you want to go back and let him throw you in jail, go ahead. But who's it going to help? McGinnis is dead. Laying in jail won't bring him back to life."

I said, "I guess not." I took the gun out of my belt and handed it over to him. "I'll buy me one next time we stop."

"Keep it until then."

He wouldn't take it from me so I stuck it back into my belt.

I followed him on down the road, trying to tell myself that my troubles were over with. I had recovered my horse and saddle and money. The whole world lay ahead of me.

But I couldn't get rid of my feeling of uneasiness. I was only seventeen years old and I'd already killed three men. I seemed to have a talent lately for getting myself into trouble that only violence would get me out of.

Maybe if I got myself a gun . . . maybe if I learned to use it and carried it, things would stop happening to me.

VI

WE TRAVELED steadily for nearly a week, not hurrying, but covering maybe twenty miles a day. We passed through a lot of towns and settlements, but in none of them could I find the gun I was looking for. I wanted one of the Navy Colts converted to take .38 cartridges. In the meantime I carried Hackett's gun stuck down in my belt. He seemed to want me to carry it.

After dark he would play his guitar and sing, but before it got dark I would practice with the gun. It was a challenge to me, I guess, trying to become expert with it. Hackett said I was a natural with a gun and maybe he was right. I'd never had any trouble hitting whatever I aimed at, provided I raised the gun to eye level and sighted it. But I also was getting so I could shoot it accurately from waist level by pointing it the way you'd point a finger. The trick, I discovered, was to keep your eye on what you wanted to hit. If you did that, the gun just naturally lined up on the same spot. By the end of the week, I could hit a three-inch rock at a dozen yards five times out of six.

The land began to change. There were fewer farms, the farther west we went, and more open grassland. Sometimes, when the wind was blowing, the grass would look like a rippling lake.

Hackett may have sensed my distrust, because he put himself out to be agreeable and gradually my distrust began to fade. I began to like the man. Once he told me a bullet had smashed his hand. He hadn't been able to hold or fire a pistol with it since.

We came to some railroad tracks and followed them on west. They led to Abilene, Hackett said, and at the prospect of seeing that famous place my excitement grew. It was too early in the season for the great herds of Texas cattle that hit Abilene every year, but it would be a lively place even without the herds.

We reached Abilene, finally, and it sure didn't disappoint me any. I counted four hotels, ten boarding houses, five general stores and ten saloons, besides all the other businesses. The buildings were different than those back in Twin Forks but they were like what I was to see farther west. One-story square buildings, for the most part, they had high false fronts that made them look bigger than they were.

Behind the buildings along the main business street were mountains of rusting tin cans and other trash, including bones. Thousands of rats lived in the dumps.

North of the tracks the respectable people lived. The part of town south of the tracks was called Texas Town because it catered to the Texas trail hands when they brought their cattle north. In Texas Town were such famous saloons as the Bull's Head, the Applejack, the Old Fruit and the Alamo. The Alamo had three sets of double glass doors and was, Hackett said, the headquarters of Wild Bill Hickok when he was in town.

He put up our horses at one of the livery stables in Texas Town. There was a sign just outside that said it was illegal to carry guns in town. The sign was hardly legible for the bullet holes in it. I asked Hackett about it and he said not to worry. He was carrying his rifle and I still had the pistol stuck down in my belt.

We went into one of the saloons. Hackett had a beer and I had sarsaparilla and we both filled a plate at the free lunch counter. Afterward we walked uptown to one of the mercantile stores. They had a whole showcase full of guns, including one of the kind I wanted to buy. For eighteen dollars I bought the gun, a holster and cartridge belt and two boxes of cartridges. I had the clerk wrap it for me because I was too self-conscious to put it on.

Hackett said it was stupid to pay just to stay in a room at the hotel when the whole prairie was out there and the weather was nice, so we laid in a stock of grub and walked to the edge of town where we set up camp in a grove of trees.

I could hardly wait to try out my new gun. I felt kind of funny when I strapped the belt around me. It was too big, so Hackett made some more holes in it and showed me how to put it around me so that it sagged low against my right leg. The reason for this, he said, was to put the gun down closer to my hand so I could get hold of it quicker when the need arose. He said lots of times out here men would fight with guns and that generally the one that lived was the one who got his gun out of the holster first. It was a carry-over from the southern dueling code, he said. The rules were that if both men drew their guns at the same time, it had to be called a fair fight and the winner couldn't be held for murder by the law.

I asked him if that was the way his hand got smashed and he said it was. He said he'd once been considered pretty good with a gun out here and down in Texas too, but since his hand got smashed he hadn't been able to hold a revolver in it, much less fire one. All he could do with his right hand anymore was strum his guitar or pull the trigger on a rifle.

The holster had a flap on it that Hackett cut off with his knife. He kept paring away at that holster until there wasn't much left of it. By the time he finished, both the grips of the gun and the trigger guard were out in the open. When you put your hand on the gun you were ready to fire at the instant it came into line.

He spent quite a bit of time getting the belt and holster to hang just right. Then he had me practice drawing it, leveling and firing it. He said, "If you carry a gun you'd better be good with it because you may have to use it now and then. But if you don't carry a gun, there are plenty of McGinnises around to make you wish you did."

I didn't need to be convinced. I'd been caught without a gun by McGinnis and I didn't have any trouble remembering how helpless I had been. I also remembered how helpless I had been back in Twin Forks until I got that rifle off one of the strangers' saddles and began shooting at them with it. I didn't intend to ever be helpless again. I figured that if a man had a gun and could use it he shouldn't have to be afraid of anything.

The practice went on and on. Finally, as the sun was going down, we built a fire and cooked supper over it. After that I laid down and went to sleep. Hackett left saying he was going up to have a couple of drinks at one of the saloons.

He woke me up about three in the morning, I suppose. It was too dark to see the face of my silver watch. Hackett was drunk and it was the first experience I'd had with someone who was. I'd seen drunks, of course, back in Twin Forks. But I'd always stayed away from them.

Hackett was shaking my shoulder. His voice was thick and he stunk of the whiskey he'd drunk. He said, "Goddamnit, Jesse, get up an' get your do's on. We're goin' back up town an' show that sonofabitch what's what."

I sat up. The air was cold and there was dew all over everything. I said, "Go to bed, Mr. Hackett. You'll feel better tomorrow when you wake up."

"The hell I will. You get your do's on, Jesse. We're goin' back uptown an' fix that sonofabitch."

"Who you talking about?"

"I'm talkin' about Sam Henry, that's who."

"What'd he do to you?"

"The sonofabitch called me a dirty four-flusher, that's what he did."

I didn't know what four-flusher meant and I didn't care. I just wanted to go back to sleep. I said, "Lemme alone. I want to go back to sleep."

"Thass what I get for helpin' you. Thass all the thanks I get. First time I need help and all you wanta do is sleep."

I said, "What do you want me to do, kill this Sam Henry for you?" I was mad and it must have showed in my voice. He didn't say anything for a minute, so I went on. This had been on my mind for a long time and now was as good a time as any to get it off. "You got something in mind for me, haven't you? All this teaching me to use a gun ain't just out of the goodness of your heart. You don't give a damn about me. You're usin' me the way you use a horse. What am I supposed to do for you when I'm good enough? You got somebody you want killed that you can't kill yourself because of that crippled hand?"

His hand, the left one, collided with the side of my face with enough force to put a brassy taste in my mouth. I got up and began to put my clothes on.

Hackett watched me until I was almost dressed. Then he asked, "What you doin', Jesse? What you goin' to do?"

I said, "I'm getting out of here. I'm going uptown and get my horse and I'm getting out of here. I don't give a damn what you do just so's you stay away from me."

He said, "Wait, Jesse. I'm sorry I hit you the way I did. I had no right."

I picked up my saddlebags and stooped to gather up my blankets. Hackett said, "Please, Jesse, for God's sake."

Most of the drunkenness seemed to be gone from him by now. "Jesse, I promise I'll never lay a hand on you again."

I said, "To hell with you."

Hackett said, "All right. I'll tell you the truth. I do want you to do something for me when you're good enough. In return I'll make you the best, Jesse. You hear? The best! You're a natural anyhow and with what I can teach you—"

I didn't stop. I started away toward town and Hackett said, "We're wanted, Jesse. Both of us. For killing McGinnis back in Cherokee."

That stopped me. "How do you know?"

"The marshal got a telegram from the deputy in Cherokee."

"What did he do, show it to you?" I stared at him suspiciously.

"He questioned me. Asked me if I was traveling with a seventeen-year-old kid."

I didn't know whether to believe him or not. The idea of being wanted by the law, a fugitive, scared me. I thought maybe I'd ought to go back to Cherokee and turn myself in, but I knew I never would. I'd done nothing wrong and I wasn't going to go to jail. I said, "If they're looking for two of us traveling together, then we should split up anyway."

"No need for splitting up. But we ought to leave."

I didn't say anything. I didn't really want to be alone. I figured I was pretty good with the gun I'd bought but I wasn't ready to try proving it. I shrugged.

"You wait here then," he said. "I'll get the horses and be right back."

He walked away into the darkness. I stared after him. He wanted me to kill somebody for him when I was good enough. He'd admitted it. I wondered who. Probably the one who had smashed his hand.

I hadn't known for sure where I was going when I left Twin Forks. I'd had a hazy idea of going to the gold mines in Colorado Territory. Now I didn't know what I was going to do.

By the time Hackett came back leading the horses I had a fire going and some coffee and bacon on. We ate, killed the fire and saddled up. When the sun came up we were half a dozen miles from Abilene. Once Hackett said, "That business in Cherokee will blow over, Jesse. After a while it will be forgotten."

I sure hoped so. I asked, "Where are we going?"

"Wouldn't be a bad idea to turn south, I'm thinking. Down that way there ain't no telegraph. It ain't likely that Cherokee business will follow us."

I said, "All right. I guess I've always wanted to see Texas anyway."

We turned south, heading for Indian Territory. It never occurred to me to doubt what Hackett said. It never occurred to me to suspect him of lying to me about the telegram. But now he spent more time teaching me to use my gun, as though there was suddenly an urgency to it that there hadn't been before.

VII

LOOKING BACK on it, I know that Hackett could never have made me into such an efficient tool for his own vengeance if I hadn't been flattered that he thought I was capable of becoming that kind of tool. I know something else I didn't realize then. He was perfectly willing to sacrifice me if necessary. He was willing to see me killed if it turned out I wasn't good enough.

I practiced constantly as we traveled south. At every settlement we bought more cartridges and when we had none to spare, I practiced my draw with an empty gun.

There were a thousand little things he impressed on me. Don't sit with your back to a window or a door. Don't turn your left side to a man you don't trust thoroughly. Don't get into any position in which it will be difficult to clear your gun. Don't get caught on horseback when your opponent is on the ground.

And other things. Don't oil your holster but

occasionally rub it with saddle soap or, if that isn't available, with ordinary laundry soap. Oil softens the leather and makes it grab. Soap dresses it but keeps it smooth. Watch the other man's eyes rather than his hands because his eyes will telegraph his intention to draw an instant before his hand begins to move. This split-second edge can save your life.

At first it had been learn to shoot, to hit what I was shooting at every time. Then it had been get the gun out quickly and smoothly, firing as it leveled into line. Now it was refine the draw. It was pare split seconds off the time it takes to draw and shoot. It was stand in such a way that the draw could begin instantly, with no preparatory movements to get into the right position for it. It was don't get caught off guard, because if your opponent suspects you may be faster than him, he most certainly will try to catch you off your guard.

Hackett was filling a place in my life that had been vacant for a long, long time. I'd never known my father. I had no memory of him at all. I suppose I had always unconsciously wanted and needed someone to fill my father's place. Grandpa had tried but he was old and besides, I'd left grandpa in Twin Forks. Hackett was the right age and he seemed intent on teaching me to defend myself, to stand secure in a world of men. Whatever his motives, he was taking a father's place with me and I accepted his counsel and tried to profit from it. I tried to be what he wanted me to be.

No older man, no mature man, can learn physical agility and skill as can a seventeen-year-old. At seventeen a boy's reflexes are as nearly perfect as they ever get. His nerves and mind are alert, his muscles strong and quick. Many times I saw amazement in Hackett's eyes at the speed with which I could draw and shoot. But he never let up on me. When he thought I was as fast as I was going to get, he said, "Jesse, it takes more than speed. Speed will only get you killed unless you hit the man you're shooting at with the first bullet out of your gun."

And another time he said, "It ain't all speed and accuracy either. A lot of it is in your mind. There are usually things said before the guns come out. If you can make the man you're facing believe you're faster than he is, you'll hurry him. And if you hurry him, there's a chance he'll miss. But never let another man hurry you. Draw the way you have learned to draw and shoot the way you've learned to shoot. If you let him make you miss your first shot, you'll be too dead to get the second off."

And again one time he said, "A gunfighter's reputation is one of the things that helps keep him alive. It makes his opponent hurry and like I told you before, hurrying is sudden death."

We crossed through Indian Territory and into Texas and a couple of days later crossed the Canadian and headed for the Red. We kept a careful eye peeled for Comanches. Hackett said they weren't very troublesome right now, but they might have trouble resisting the temptation to attack two lone white men. It was early May and we were a hundred miles south of the Red River when we ran into the first of the Texas herds trailing north.

I doubt if I'll ever forget the sight of it. We topped a flat mesa and there they were in front of us, at least three thousand head in one great herd. At first we could see only fifty or so cattle and the point rider and behind a monstrous cloud of dust. But as the herd drew closer the flank riders on the near side became visible and as the breeze drifted the cloud of dust temporarily to one side, we could see the full extent of the herd and of the remuda being driven along parallel to its course.

We sat motionless on the mesa rim, but before long we were spotted and three riders came trotting toward us. They hauled in a dozen yards away and stared at us watchfully.

The man in the lead was about fifty, I supposed. He was a big, bony man, with a craggy, rawboned face. He had a couple of days growth of whiskers on his dark-tanned face and a graying mustache. His hair hadn't seen a barber's shears for at least two months. His eyes were the same blue as the sky, but they were plenty hard as they looked us up and down. He asked, "You two alone?"

Hackett and I both nodded. The man said, "I'm

hiring if you want to work. I lost three men in a stampede a week ago and I'm short-handed. Pay's thirty dollars between here and Abilene. If you quit before we get to Abilene you get nothing. If you're fired you get paid for the days you've worked."

I looked at Hackett. I wanted to take the job and I knew we didn't have to go all the way into Abilene. I was used to working and the idea of working with cattle appealed to me. I noticed the man eyeing my low-slung gun. He was also eyeing Hackett's crippled hand.

Hackett hesitated. When he didn't speak, I said, "We'll take the job. I'm no hand with cattle, but I figure I can learn."

He shifted his glance from Hackett to me when I spoke. "You help Slim Gray with the remuda. Keep that gun in its holster. I want no trouble. You understand?"

I nodded without saying anything. He looked at Hackett. "You take the drag. Tell MacPhee to report to me."

Hackett nodded. The man rode close and stuck out his hand. He smiled but the coldness never left his eyes. "I'm Francisco Ross. These are my cattle. Work hard for me and you've got a job on the home place down south if that's what you want."

I took his hand and his grip was hard and firm without trying to crush my hand. Hackett shook hands with him too. Ross turned away and trotted his horse back toward the herd, his two men following. Hackett headed for the tail end of the herd and I headed for the remuda.

There were fifty or sixty horses in the bunch, being driven along by a kid about my age and a younger one. I figured Slim Gray would be the older one so I rode to him. I said, "Mr. Ross hired me and told me to report to you."

He was a tall, stringy kid with yellow hair and eyes that were the same gray Hackett's were. His skin was bright red from the sun and peeling. He was one of those unlucky people who never tan, but who only burn. He stuck out a hand to me and said, "I'm Gray. They call me Slim." He jerked his head toward the younger boy. "That's Billy. Billy Ross. He's the boss's kid."

I nodded and he said, "Just keep the horses moving and keep 'em bunched."

I nodded again. He turned his horse and rode away. I got over between the horses and the cattle and held a position there. It wasn't any trouble keeping them bunched. They were trail-wise and knew what was expected of them. The dust was the hard part of the job. I hadn't been with the remuda fifteen minutes before I was completely covered by a fine layer of dust. It choked my nose and lungs. It made grit in my mouth and grated between my teeth. It got into my eyes and I had to keep rubbing them all the time. Slim Gray had moved over to the windward side of the bunch where there wasn't any dust, but I didn't resent it or even think about it much. I was new so it was natural they'd give me the dirtiest work to do.

Riding along, I had plenty of time to think. I'd never thought much before about what I was going to do with my life. I didn't know what line of work I intended on following. I had a grade-school education that I'd gotten in St. Louis while I was living with my aunt. But I didn't know how to do anything but work in a store.

When I left home I'd intended on going to Colorado to look for gold. Now it didn't look like I'd see Colorado. Not for a long time at least. I wondered why Hackett hadn't objected to going back to Abilene. If we were wanted there it seemed funny he'd be willing to go back so soon, and I hadn't mentioned us not having to go all the way. For the first time I wondered if he'd told me the truth, if we really were wanted in Abilene.

In the afternoon the heat and the dust grew worse. The stink of cattle and horses did too. Yet in spite of dust and heat, in spite of the smell, I was enjoying myself. Working on horseback sure beat working with your back and hands the way I had at Blumenthal's. Thinking about Blumenthal's made me remember grandpa and Julia and I was suddenly homesick for them. But then I thought of Julia's father and Blumenthal and the other townspeople in Twin Forks and I didn't want to go back.

About an hour before sundown, the herd was halted where a narrow stream wound through a thick grove of stunted trees. There was a canvas-topped wagon already there and an old man with a white beard had a fire going and was cooking supper over it. Gray and Billy Ross and I bunched the horses in the trees upstream from the herd but below the camp. There was plenty of grass there, and after drinking the horses spread out and began to graze. Slim rode to me and said, "Keep 'em bunched but not too close. Billy and I will eat and then I'll relieve you so you can eat." All the time he was talking he was looking at my gun kind of enviously, as if he wished he had one too.

VIII

SLIM AND Billy rode away toward the chuckwagon. I was scared for a few minutes at the responsibility of holding the horses bunched until they got back, but the horses were quiet and didn't seem to want to do anything but graze. After half an hour or so, Slim came back and told me to go in and eat.

Most of the men had already eaten. I went to the chuckwagon and got a tin plate and a knife and fork. The cook ladled the plate full of stew from a pot simmering over the fire and I took a couple of biscuits from a pan. I put the plate down and went back for a tin cup that I filled with coffee.

Hackett wasn't anywhere around. I supposed he was with the cattle. Either he had already eaten or he hadn't yet been relieved. I squatted on my heels, remembering instinctively what Hackett had told me about turning my left side to anyone.

I heard a voice: "Pretty damn fancy riggin' for a kid. Your daddy know you're packin' a big black gun like that?" The voice was taunting and unpleasant. I looked up.

The man talking was about Hackett's age. He was big and bony and had a week's growth of whiskers on his face. He had the coldest eyes I'd ever seen. One of the other men said, "Stop it, Len. Let him alone. He just signed on today and the boss wouldn't have hired him if he wasn't needing him."

"I ain't hurtin' him. Just seems to me he's puffin' on mighty big. Somebody ought to take that gun away from him an'—"

He reminded me of McGinnis. There was something about his eyes, something deliberately mean, like he wanted to hurt somebody just for the fun of it.

I said, "You want to try taking it away?"

I was surprised at myself for saying that. It had just slipped out. But when it did, something flared in his eyes and his mouth looked even uglier than it had before. He took a step toward me. "Somebody should teach you some manners, kid."

He was wearing a gun but I didn't figure he'd use it. At least not until I did. He was too contemptuous of me to be on guard.

I put my plate on the ground in front of me along with my coffee cup. I stood up.

He didn't stop, and I knew what he meant to do. He was going to beat me with his fists the way McGinnis had. I said, "Don't come any closer, mister. I'll have to kill you if you do."

He stopped. His expression was puzzled as though he didn't know whether to take me seriously or laugh out loud. I said, "I don't know what this is all about, but neither you nor nobody else is going to put his hands on me."

He hesitated a moment. The man who had spoken before said, "For Christ's sake, Len, leave him be."

"Huh uh," said Len. "Not now."

I said, "Then go for your gun. But don't come any closer."

He took another step toward me and I pulled my gun, not hurrying. The hammer cocked as the gun lined up, pointing straight at his belly.

He was off balance and taken by surprise. The other man now stepped between the two of us. He had his back to me and was facing Len. He said, "You dumb sonofabitch, a gunshot is all we need. Them cattle still ain't quieted down from that stampede a week ago."

Len growled something I didn't hear. He swung around and walked away.

I slid my gun back into the holster. The other man turned and looked at me. He said, "Don't be so touchy, kid. He was just funnin' you."

"That ain't my idea of fun."

"He wouldn't have hurt you."

I said, "I ran into one like him a month ago. He purty near beat me to death before he quit."

He said, "That gun will get you into a lot more trouble than it'll ever get you out of, son. Take my word for that. Better take it off."

His eyes were steady and his face was calm. I suddenly felt ashamed. I said, "I'm sorry. I didn't mean to be smart. But I'm not giving up my gun."

He shrugged and turned away. I looked around for Len but I didn't see him anywhere. I squatted down and began to eat again. I was surprised that my hand was steady. I hadn't been afraid of Len. I'd known I could kill him any time I wanted to. I had a moment's uneasiness. I was changing and I wasn't sure I liked the change. I was young but I was old enough to know that nobody should feel so sure of his own ability to kill any other men he might come up against.

But whether I wanted to admit it or not, I liked the feeling of power my skill with a gun was giving me. Maybe I liked it too damn much. It was pleasant not being afraid of anyone.

Hackett rode into camp and dismounted. The boss, Francisco Ross, followed him. He looked at me. "Take the first turn night-herdin' the horses, Jesse. Slim will relieve you around midnight."

I nodded and got to my feet. I walked to the chuckwagon and put my dishes in the wreck pan, where I'd seen the other men put theirs. I went to my horse and swung to his back. I rode out into the darkness in the direction I'd come from earlier.

I knew the boss would hear about the argument I'd had with Len. He might fire me when he did, even though it hadn't been my fault. He couldn't risk trouble in camp and he couldn't risk gunshots that would make the cattle run.

I knew something else. If I stayed I would have more trouble with Len. Like McGinnis, he was a bully who got pleasure out of tormenting people weaker than he was. I'd have more trouble with Len and I'd probably have to kill him before we got to Abilene.

I should have thrown my gun away that night. I should have taken the beating Len wanted to inflict on me. It would have been easier. It would have saved me a lot of grief.

The herd covered about a dozen miles a day. Each morning it took almost an hour to get it lined out heading north. The cattle loafed along, grazing as they went. I traveled with the horses, usually on the windward flank. The chuckwagon pulled out early in the morning, passed the slowly moving herd and stopped where it had been decided to camp for the night.

I had no more trouble with Len for several days but I caught him watching me and scowling several times. Mr. Ross had heard about the trouble between us and he told me that if I pulled my gun again I could draw my pay and leave. I asked him if a man wasn't entitled to defend himself and he said sure, but not with a gun. I told him Len was half again as big as me and he said for me to stay away from him, then. But his expression said he knew I had a problem that talk wasn't going to solve. He knew Len a whole lot better than I did. He knew Len was a bully and knew Len wouldn't quit.

We swam the cattle across the Red River even though it was running bank-full from rains up near its source. I nearly got swept downstream when a floating tree dragged my horse under. I managed to get clear and grabbed onto a loose horse's tail and let him pull me out on the bank. I got another horse and rode downstream. About five miles down I found old Duke. He'd managed to drag himself out on the bank but he was dead from a big hole in his side where a broken tree branch had penetrated. I got my saddle off him and left him there, feeling kind of sad because he'd been a link between me and home. When I got back to the herd, Mr. Ross gave me another horse for my own to take his place.

I liked Mr. Ross and I was determined not to let Len force me into a gunfight with him. But Len kept tormenting me and trying to egg me on. He made nasty remarks to me every time he got the chance. At last, when we were a week north of the Red River, I had enough. I said, "Len, you want a fight with me so much it's a bad taste in your mouth. I don't want any gunshots making the cattle run but I sure ain't afraid of you. If you want to ride over into those hills with me tonight after we make camp, then we can get this over with."

He said he'd be ready when I was. That evening as soon as we made camp, I went to Mr. Ross and said, "Len keeps pushing, Mr. Ross, and I'd just as soon get it over with. I told him I'd ride out into those hills with him tonight."

He started to tell me I couldn't, then stopped himself. He said, "All right, Jesse. You take Hackett with you to make sure Len don't pull anything."

I nodded. I found Hackett and we rode off away from the herd with Len and another man he'd got to go with him. I remembered the stories I'd read about duels, where both men had seconds and where they met at dawn in some foggy grove of trees and shot it out. This was some different but the idea was the same. I knew one of us, either Len or me, wouldn't be coming back. Hackett had his rifle along and the man with Len wore a revolver in a holster at his side. He was a friend of Len's, or at least as close to a friend as Len had, being the unpleasant kind of character he was.

We rode for about two miles, not saying much. Len kept glancing back at me, studying my face. If he'd catch my glance he'd grin at me like he was really going to enjoy killing me, but as we kept going his grin got a little strained. He was beginning to wonder if he hadn't bit off more than he could chew. I didn't look scared, so he was wondering if I wasn't faster than he had thought. That other time I hadn't really drawn my gun, I'd just taken it out of the holster and pointed it at him.

Finally Hackett said, "This is far enough. This here is a good level spot." He stopped his horse and got to the ground. I swung down and Hackett took the reins of my horse. Len's friend, whose name was Gus, took the reins of Len's horse and his own. Len said to him, "Watch Hackett, Gus. I don't want no bullet in the back."

I looked at Hackett. "How's this going to be? I'm not going to turn my back on him."

Hackett said, "All right. Face each other. Back away a step at a time. When I yell, 'Now!', you both draw and shoot."

I said, "All right." Hackett looked at Len. "That suit you all right?"

"Suits me." He tried to grin at me but it didn't quite come off.

Hackett said, "Start backing off. A step at a time."

I glanced at him. I knew he was going to yell when Len was off balance. I said, "You do this right, Mr. Hackett. I don't need any edge."

He nodded but I didn't know if he'd do what I'd told him to. I kept backing away a step at a time, timing my steps exactly with Len's so that Hackett couldn't yell when Len was off balance and I wasn't. I wasn't afraid of Len. I knew I could beat him and I didn't want to feel guilty when it was over with.

We kept backing away, a step at a time until about fifty feet separated us. I could see Len getting more nervous all the time as the distance between us increased. He was probably better at short-range than he was at long-range shooting, I supposed.

I thought I was ready and listening for Hackett's yell, but it caught me a little off guard just the same. I started, realizing I'd been thinking about Len instead of staying completely relaxed. I saw Len grab frantically for his gun. His hand was on the grips before mine even moved.

But this was wholly automatic with me. A thousand times, ten thousand times in the past few months my hand had snaked to the gun grips at my side. My gun was out of its holster and the hammer was back before Len's had even cleared.

I could have stopped myself and I would have stopped if Len had quit right then. But he didn't quit. There was flat terror in his eyes when he saw how fast I was, when he realized he was going to lose. But his hand kept coming up and his gun kept coming into line. . . .

I knew I'd waited long enough. My gun was level and the hammer was at full cock. Hackett yelled, "Jesse! Shoot!"

The gun bucked against my palm. The feel was

familiar and I knew where the slug had gone even before I saw it take effect. Len grunted loudly and took a backward step as though to maintain balance. His gun, not yet in line, fired as reflex tightened his finger on the trigger. The bullet tore into the ground six feet in front of me and a little to one side. It ricocheted away, whining, into space.

Len seemed to be trying desperately to stand up. His gun now hung limply at his side. A red stain was spreading across the front of his shirt. He put his left hand up to it, then took the hand away and looked at it. Only then, when he saw his bloody palm, did he realize what had happened to him. Only then did he realize he was going to die.

He sat down suddenly. He managed to keep his body erect for almost half a minute before he toppled over to one side. After that he didn't move.

Gus was saying breathlessly, "Holy Jesus Christ! I never seen anything move so fast in my whole damn life. Holy Jesus Christ!"

Last time I'd killed a man I'd felt like vomiting. I didn't feel like that this time. I just felt drained, of strength, of all my energy. I looked at Hackett. "Help Gus load him on his horse and bring him back to camp."

I got on my own horse and rode away alone. I didn't want to talk to anyone. I wanted to be alone, to think. I didn't even realize that I'd given Hackett an order. I didn't even realize that our roles had changed.

IX

Len was the fourth man I killed and I never even knew what his last name was. I rode back to camp leaving Gus and Hackett to load Len's body and bring it in. Some of the trail hands were in camp, including the one who'd tried to stop my first fight with Len. They all knew what had happened when they saw me come in alone. They knew Len was dead.

There was something funny about the way they looked at me. I didn't know it then but that look was something I was going to have to get used to. It was a look in which fear and dislike were mixed. It was the way respectable people would always look at me when they found out who I was and what I'd done.

I guess that night it went to my head. I was, after all, only seventeen years old. I went to the fire and got myself a plate of stew. I got some coffee and biscuits and found myself a place to sit and eat. Nobody spoke to me or came near to me.

I'd almost finished eating when I saw Gus and Hackett coming, leading Len's horse with his body laid across the saddle face-down, and tied so it wouldn't slip. Francisco Ross detailed two men to dig a grave. The rest of the men stood not far from where the grave was being dug. Gus was talking to them, telling them how fast my draw had been.

He'd never seen anything like it, he said, and he'd seen a few of the famous ones. He said I was faster than Wild Bill ever was. That had to have been an exaggeration, but he was enjoying the attention he was getting from the crew. He didn't seem upset that Len was dead and I supposed he hadn't been a particularly close friend of Len's after all.

After a while Ross walked over to me. I had finished eating so I got up. He said, "Whether you know it or not, you're hooked. By the time Gus gets through telling how fast you are in Abilene, you'll have half the gunslicks in the country wanting to try you out."

I didn't say anything. There didn't seem to be anything I could say. He went on, "Len pushed you into it, so I'm not going to fire you. You can stay with the herd until we get to Abilene."

I said, "Thanks, Mr. Ross." I was irritated at him and I suppose it showed. He was letting me stay on like it was a favor. He was saying on the one hand that killing Len hadn't been my fault, but he was plainly thinking I could have avoided it if I'd really wanted to.

What was I supposed to do, I wondered sourly. Was I supposed to let anyone who wanted to beat me up? I didn't admit to myself that if I hadn't been packing a low-slung gun, Len wouldn't have bothered to notice me.

The herd trailed north. Slim Gray and Billy Ross treated me differently now, like I was somebody.

They stayed in the dust and let me ride on the windward side. I wasn't asked to stand night guard.

I wasn't sure whether I liked being treated like that or not. I enjoyed it in a way. I enjoyed being important. I enjoyed having men look at me with awe and fear. But something bothered me. I puzzled about it and finally decided what it was about their expressions that troubled me. They looked at me the way they looked at a rattlesnake, with respect, but with fear and hatred.

Even Hackett seemed different. He didn't treat me like a boy any more. He treated me like a man.

In Abilene, we drove the cattle directly into the loading pens, ours being the first herd to arrive. When the gates slammed shut on the last of them, we trooped toward the saloons. The men were dusty and grimy and soaked with sweat. They were long-haired and bewhiskered, and they were laughing and yelling and cuffing each other good-naturedly. I looked at Hackett. I said, "You lied about the marshal here getting a telegram from Cherokee. You just didn't want me to leave."

He didn't deny it and I didn't push it. There wasn't any use. We went into the Bull's Head and the crew ordered drinks. The bartender shook his head when he came to me, but Gus took over. "Know who this kid is, bartender?"

"No, why should I?"

"Well if you don't now, you will. He's the fastest gun alive, that's what he is. His name's Jesse Hand. He's seventeen years old and he's already killed four men."

"What am I supposed to do, get down on my knees to him?" The bartender was irritated, but he was looking at me with that familiar expression in his eyes.

"You could start by giving him a drink."

The bartender came and stood in front of me. "All right kid, what do you want?"

"Beer will do."

He drew a beer and slid it down the bar to me. I picked it up and took a drink of it. I didn't like the taste, but it was better than whiskey. I'd tasted whiskey by draining the last few drops out of a bottle once back home, the way Charlie Two Horses had.

Gus was telling how fast I was again. There were several local men in the saloon and they kept glancing at me speculatively, as if they didn't know whether to believe Gus or not.

Mr. Ross had told me every gunslick in the country would want to try me out. I wondered when it would start. I realized I was standing at the bar the way Hackett had taught me to stand, with plenty of space between my right hand and the man next to me, with someone I trusted thoroughly on my left, Hackett himself right now.

I turned my head, "Let's get a room at the hotel.

I want a bath and shave. I want to put on some clean clothes for a change "

He nodded and we left. As we stepped out into the street, I could still hear Gus telling the crowd how fast I was. Hackett said sourly, "He's off, the sonofabitch. By the time he gets through telling it, your hand will be so fast it can't even be seen by the human eye. By night, three or four local bully boys will be waiting at the Bull's Head for you to show."

"Maybe we ought to leave."

"Maybe. But by God we're going to have a bath, a good meal and a good night's sleep before we do. We've earned that much."

We got a room at one of the hotels and had a couple of baths sent up. They consisted of two big wooden tubs and a number of buckets of hot water to fill them with. Hackett and I got in those tubs and soaked until I thought we were going to dissolve. Then we got out, shaved, and dressed in the clean clothes we'd bought before we went up to the room. After that we found the best-looking restaurant in town and had ourselves a meal. I was already wondering if it wouldn't be smart of me to take off my gun.

Two things prevented me. Pride for one. I was proud to be called the "fastest gun alive" even if it wasn't true. Caution for another. If Gus did promote a fight for me the way Hackett said he would, then I'd be pretty stupid to get caught without my gun. Plenty of men in Abilene would love to batter the "fastest gun alive" into insensibility with their fists if they ever caught him without his gun.

I saw some women in the restaurant, and a girl about my age. She made me think of Julia and I suddenly felt awfully homesick for Julia and for grandpa and for the house we'd lived in there. I made up my mind I'd go back for Julia before very long. Maybe Hackett and I could go to Colorado when we left Abilene. Maybe we could find gold. As soon as I had a little stake, I could go back for Julia.

The town marshal came in while we were eating. He came over to our table and stood there looking down. He said, "Guns aren't allowed in Abilene."

Hackett said, "That ordinance ain't enforced."

The marshal said, "I'm enforcing it now. I'm starting with you two."

The other people in the restaurant were looking at us. Hackett said, "We ain't giving up our guns. Not until you got the guns from everybody else."

There was a stubbornness about the marshal's jaw. Hackett's eyes were equally stubborn. I knew if the marshal kept pushing and Hackett kept refusing, there was going to be trouble and I knew who would have to do the shooting when the chips were down. Me. Hackett wasn't near fast enough with his rifle and besides, it was leaning against a chair nearly out of his reach.

I didn't want any shooting here. The marshal was the law and he had a right to take our guns. I didn't figure it was safe to give mine up but I didn't want to have to kill him over it.

I said, "What if we was to leave town right away? Would that be all right?"

He hesitated a minute. He looked at the way I wore my gun. And suddenly I knew he'd heard Gus's stories about how fast I was. He nodded. "You got an hour to get out of town."

He turned his back and went toward the door. Hackett reached for the rifle but I said, "No. Leave it be. If he turns his head and sees you reaching for that, I'll have to kill him."

He let his hand drop. Sure enough the marshal turned his head and looked at us as he opened the door.

I stared at Hackett. He'd taught me to shoot and he'd taught me to draw. He'd said I was a natural and I'd learned my lessons well. But there was more to it than practice and he knew that as well as I. Part of the training had to be for real. I had to stand face to face with other men, and shoot it out with them, and learn to kill before I would be the tool Hackett wanted me to be.

He would have forced the marshal to draw. He'd have done it deliberately if I hadn't told him to stop. The cold-bloodedness of it was a shock to me. I said, "That's the reason you reached for your rifle, isn't it? You knew he'd turn his head before he went out the door. You knew he'd draw and you knew I'd have to kill him if he did."

He asked, "Is that all you think of me? After all I've done for you?" He was acting hurt but I knew it was just an act.

I said, "If you try to set up anything else like that, I'm through with you."

"Set up anything else like what? All I did was reach for my rifle. We were leaving. What was wrong with that?"

There was no use answering. We got up and left. We went to the hotel and got our things and paid the bill. Mr. Ross had given us each thirty dollars and we both had more than twenty of it left. We went to the livery stable and got our horses. The marshal went past making his rounds as we came out of the livery barn.

He drew his horse to a halt. He looked at me. "Good thing you're leaving, son. There are three or four local boys who fancy themselves gunslingers waiting for you already up at the Bull's Head Saloon."

Hackett said, "Maybe you ought to accommodate them, Jesse, before we leave."

The marshal looked at him. "You're the one that's pushing him, aren't you? Why? Because of that smashed hand of yours?"

Hackett said, "Go to hell."

The marshal said, "I'd be doing this boy a favor if I threw you into jail. You'll get him killed."

I said, "Don't try it, marshal."

He looked at me. "You ain't going to take any advice but I'm going to give some to you anyway. Get rid of that gun. You're young enough so that you can forget everything you know about using it. That loudmouth up at the Bull's Head can't hurt you once you're out of town. But there's a loud-mouth just like him in every town you'll hit. And if you're as good as he says you are, you'll be known all over the country inside a year."

Hackett said, "Come on, Jesse. We can get all the sermons we want in church."

He rode away and I followed him. I turned my head and looked back at the marshal sitting his horse in the middle of the street. He was solid and strong and I couldn't forget the way his eyes had looked as he talked to me.

I knew I should take his advice. But I also knew I would not. The prospect of being somebody important and famous was too much for me to resist.

X

WE RODE straight west out of Abilene, following the Smoky Hill River, which had its source in Colorado, Hackett said. He was putting himself out to be agreeable with me. He probably sensed that I wanted to pull away from him. Nobody likes the feeling they are being used and I was no exception to that rule.

This was Indian country, so we stayed watchful as we rode. Now and then we found the tracks of unshod horses and sometimes the remains of a fire, and once we saw a file of mounted warriors silhouetted against the skyline half a mile away.

It was midsummer now, and the days were hot and still. In the afternoon, great puffy thunderheads piled up in the west and came sailing east, and sometimes we'd be pelted by a downpour or battered savagely by hail. Several times lightning struck near enough so that we could smell sulphur in the air.

The country was rich with game—antelope, deer and buffalo. We were across the boundary and in Colorado Territory when we encountered the first buffalo hunters we had seen.

They were camped in a little draw beside a narrow stream. They had five wagons drawn up in a circle. They had a fair-sized herd of mules and saddle horses. Dry hides were piled six or eight feet high in the circle formed by the wagons.

We smelled the camp as we rode in. The stench was almost overpowering, the sweetish sick smell of rotting flesh. I got a whiff of it and said, "Hell, let's go on. I don't want to stop down there."

Hackett said, "We can get meat from them and maybe cartridges. We don't have to stay."

We rode into the hunters' camp, approaching from upwind. Three hunters came out to meet us, rifles in their hands.

They were a shaggy, unwashed lot. All three had beards and their hair was long on their necks and around their ears. Their clothes were slick with grease and blood and when the wind shifted a little, we caught their smell. It was as bad as that of the hides. I wondered how they could eat with that stink in their noses all the time.

Hackett said, "Howdy. This here's Jesse Hand and I'm Ben Hackett. We thought maybe you could spare some meat and that maybe you'd have some ca'tridges you'd sell to us."

One of the hunters, a heavy-set man with black hair and a black beard, said, "Git down. We can't spare no ca'tridges but you can have all the meat you want. You out of Abilene?"

Hackett nodded.

"Rails any further west than Abilene?"

"They've reached Ellsworth. They expectin' a hundred thousand cattle in Ellsworth this year an' next."

"Then we won't have so far to haul these hides."

"You ready to go on in?"

"Purt near. We got four wagonloads. One more an' we'll go in with 'em." The man was looking at me, now, studying the way I wore my gun. There was interest in his face, the same interest I had seen in other faces back at the Bull's Head in Abilene. He looked away from me and looked at Hackett again. "Who's the sprout and what's he wearin' his gun that way for?"

Hackett said, "The sprout is Jesse Hand and he can put three bullets in your heart while you're getting your gun clear. Want to try him out?"

I said, "Now just wait a minute, Mr. Hackett. Nobody's going to try me out. All we want is meat and cartridges."

The black-bearded man looked at me again. "Seein' a kid wearin' a gun like that just naturally makes a man wonder whether he's as good as he thinks he is."

Hackett said, "He's as good."

Right then a couple of Indians rode out of the trees along the stream bed and came toward us. Both were young and both had paint on their faces and their naked chests. They carried rifles in their hands. They were scowling.

They halted their horses about a dozen yards away and began pointing at the hides and jabbering angrily at the black-bearded man. He had turned away from us and pointed his rifle at them. All of a sudden he fired it without warning and one of the Indians fell out of his saddle and hit the ground. The other whirled his horse and started to gallop away. The black-bearded man raised his rifle and sighted carefully on the Indian's back.

The Indians hadn't done anything but talk. Killing the first one had been cold-blooded murder and I didn't intend to stand by and see the other one murdered the same way. Before I hardly knew what I was doing, my gun was in my hand and firing and the black-bearded man folded forward and collapsed to the ground.

The other two whirled back toward me, bringing their rifles up. I fired again and a second one went down. Before I could get the third one, Hackett's rifle roared and the third buffalo hunter slammed against the wagon behind him with a crash.

The Indian had disappeared. The one on the ground was dead. I looked toward the trees lining the creek and Hackett said, "I think we'd better get the hell out of here. There could be fifty Indians in those trees down there."

I stared at the three hunters. One was stirring but the other two were dead. It didn't seem decent to leave them lying there, but I knew it would be foolish of us to stay.

We turned and rode away, with neither the meat nor the cartridges.

At the crest of the next rise I turned in my saddle and looked behind. Two more hunters were riding down into the hunters' camp. One of them dismounted beside the bodies on the ground. He looked up and saw us at the top of the ridge. He raised his gun and I saw smoke puff from it. The heavy slug kicked up dust on the slope below us about a hundred yards away. An instant after it struck, I heard the gun's report.

Hackett spurred his horse and I followed him. The toll was mounting rapidly, I thought. I had now killed six men and I still wasn't quite eighteen. Furthermore, those hunters would probably follow us. If they couldn't catch up with us, they'd report us to the law. One of the hunters we'd shot had still been alive. He might stay alive long enough to give them a description of us. They'd even know our names.

I looked at Hackett's face. It was calm and untroubled. I said, "You'd like to make an outlaw out of me, wouldn't you?"

He said, "Don't blame me for what happened back there. I didn't have a thing to do with it."

"You were trying to get a fight going when those Indians butted in. You've had plenty to do with everything that's happened to me since the first day I ran into you. You deliberately followed me from Twin Forks when you heard I'd killed those two men because you figured you had a use for me."

Hackett didn't deny it. I said, "The marshal in Abilene was right. He said you were pushing me. And he said you'd get me killed. But he was wrong. I'm pulling out right now. You can go your way and I'll go mine."

I turned my horse and headed north. I didn't know what was up that way and I didn't care. I didn't even look back to see if he was following.

I'd ridden maybe half a mile. Suddenly I heard a gunshot back of me and turned my head. I saw Hackett's horse galloping with Hackett leaning low over his neck. About a quarter-mile behind him there were half a dozen Indians. I don't know whether they thought Hackett was one of the buffalo hunters or whether they were just stirred up enough to try killing any white man they found.

I wanted to leave him but I couldn't leave this way. I owed him something for helping me catch McGinnis and get my horse and money back. I owed him for teaching me to use a gun. I whirled my horse and dug spurs into his sides.

I didn't head straight for Hackett but for a spot about a mile ahead of him. I could see little puffs of smoke coming from the Indians' guns but Hackett wasn't wasting lead. At that range, shooting from the back of a running horse, there wasn't one chance in a thousand of hitting anything.

I didn't seem able to gain on either Hackett or the Indians, but I did get closer because our courses slowly converged. At last, after about half an hour's hard riding, I was only a couple of hundred yards to Hackett's right, and maybe three hundred yards ahead of the Indians. I figured if Hackett and me could join up we could reach cover of some kind and make a stand.

I kept bearing left so that I could join up with him. The Indians had stopped firing. They'd probably emptied their guns. One of them, though, had a repeating rifle that he was apparently able to reload on the back of a running horse. He was busy reloading now.

Behind this bunch of Indians I saw more coming, maybe a mile farther back. It was a good thing I'd returned or Hackett wouldn't have had a chance. But maybe neither of us had a chance. If these Indians didn't get us, the other bunch would. And if they didn't get us, then the buffalo hunters probably would. All in all, things didn't look too good.

Right then, the Indian with the repeater began firing again. His second shot struck Hackett and he flopped forward and threw his arms around his horse's neck.

I reined over hard and pulled my horse up alongside of his. I yelled, "Hackett, is it bad?"

He turned his head and looked at me. He was almost gray and there was sweat all over his face. I turned in my saddle, drawing my revolver as I did. I shot at the pursuing Indians' horses instead of shooting at the Indians themselves. I wanted to stop them more than I wanted to kill any of them.

One of their horses fell, throwing his rider clear. Another veered aside, stung by a bullet I guess, and began to buck. The other Indians hauled their horses in.

Just then we reached a shallow wash and I yanked both our horses to a halt. Hackett fell out of the saddle. I caught him before he hit the ground and dragged him into the wash. I flopped down beside him, frantically punching empties out of my gun, reloading afterward. The horses ran a ways beyond the wash and stopped uncertainly.

Hackett's rifle was still in his saddle boot and of no use to us. All I had was my revolver and a beltful of cartridges.

I didn't waste any trying to scare the Indians. I shoved the gun back into its holster and turned Hackett over on his back. There was a stain of blood as big as my hand on his chest. I unbuttoned his shirt and looked at the wound. Little bubbles of blood came from the hole every time he breathed. Hackett wasn't going any further. I knew that. He was going to die right here.

It seemed ironic after we'd risked our necks to save that Indian's life that we'd be killed by his Indian friends. Hackett said, "I'm going to die, Jesse. I'm going to die."

I nodded.

He laughed a little, but stopped as a spasm of pain crossed his face. "Ain't that a hell of a thing. Killed by a goddam Indian."

I didn't say anything. I was plenty scared. I was surrounded by hostile Indians with a man who was going to die in a little while and leave me all alone.

Hackett was watching me. "Thanks for coming back."

I nodded, staring toward the Indians. They were having a powwow back there about two hundred yards away. They were well out of the range of my gun, and for the moment they weren't shooting at us. I glanced right and left. The shallow wash we were in was as crooked as a dog's hind leg. All the

Indians had to do was get down into the wash on both sides and they could crawl unseen to within about fifty feet. What they didn't know was that when they got that close I had a big advantage over them.

Hackett groaned and moved. He looked at me with a kind of desperation in his eyes. "There was a reason I taught you how to use a gun. I wanted you to kill somebody for me. I still want you to."

I didn't answer him. I wondered why the hell he couldn't just die in peace. Why did he have to reach out for his vengeance from the grave?

He said, "Jesse, you owe it to me."

Still I didn't say anything. When I left him I was going to put my gun away. I wasn't going to wear it again, provided I got out of this mess alive.

Hackett said, "Jesse, please. I been living for this a long, long time. He deserves to die. He didn't smash my hand with a bullet. He did it with his gun. He knocked me cold and while I was out he put my hand on a block of wood and battered it to a pulp with the butt of his gun."

I felt a little sick to my stomach thinking about it. I asked, "What's his name and where will he be?"

"His name's Sol Justin. You'll find him at a place called Julesburg Station north of here and near the Colorado line."

For a while I didn't say anything. I didn't want to fight Hackett's fights for him. But his eyes were pleading with me and I could tell he was holding on to life, waiting for me to say I would.

I nodded. "All right. I'll get him for you."

He said, "You swear it, Jesse? You promise me?"

"I promise."

He nodded slightly and closed his eyes. He drew in one great breath and exhaled it. Then he died. He never drew another breath.

I stared at the Indians They had been joined by the second bunch I'd seen farther back. It didn't matter that I'd promised to kill Hackett's enemy. I wasn't going to have to do it. I was going to die right here.

XI

I COULDN'T understand why the Indians' powwow was lasting so long. They seemed to be arguing. Now and then one or another of them would look toward me. They had no way of knowing Hackett was dead. They were too far away to tell. I supposed some of them wanted to keep on trying to kill us and the others wanted to give it up.

At last they stopped arguing. They mounted and galloped away without a backward glance. It occurred to me that maybe the Indian whose life I'd saved in the buffalo hunters' camp had talked them out of killing me.

I waited a while to see if they'd come back. I wanted to bury Hackett but I had no tools to do it with. Finally I carried him to a place in the wash where there was a steep bank and pulled earth down over him with my hands. It wasn't a very satisfactory way to bury him but it was the best I could do. I left his saddle there on the ground but I took his horse and rifle and saddle scabbard along with me.

The Indians seemed to have gone for good so I mounted up and headed north, leading Hackett's horse. I'd just as well get Hackett's vengeance over with but I promised myself that as soon as I had, I was going to put away my gun and try to get a job. I didn't like the way the damn gun got me into trouble every place I went.

It was lonely out there on the plains. The loneliness bothered me, but I wasn't afraid. I figured I could handle anything that came along.

I kept going for three days until I struck the South Platte. I turned upstream and hadn't gone more than half a dozen miles before I came to a stage road. I followed that and came into Julesburg just as the sun was going down.

It was a pretty sorry-looking town. It had more shacks in it than buildings and at the edge of it there were half a dozen Indian tepees.

There was no livery stable but there was a public corral. I took my horses there and left them, then walked to the nearest saloon. There seemed to be more saloons in town than anything.

This one was a smelly place built of logs. It had

sawdust three inches deep on the floor. Along one wall ran the bar.

There were maybe half a dozen men in the place besides the bartender. I felt nervous but I went up to the bar as if I owned the place. I said, "I'm looking for Sol Justin."

The man behind the bar had long hair and a full beard. He said, "He ain't here, kid. What do you want him for?"

I figured the truth would smoke Justin out faster than beating around the bush. I said, "I'm going to kill him."

The bartender stared at me unbelievingly. He didn't seem to know whether to laugh or not. At last he said, "That might take some doin', kid."

I asked, "Where can I find him? Do you know?"

"He'll likely be in here after a while. I don't know where the hell he is right now."

"What's he do? For a living?"

The bartender laughed. "Ask him, sonny. Before you kill him, I mean."

The other men were staring at me, staring at my gun. For once, none of them made any remarks about it. Maybe there were others in Julesburg as young as I who packed a gun. Or maybe I was beginning to look a little less green than I had when I first began wearing it.

I ordered beer and the bartender didn't give me any argument. He slid it down the bar to me and I paid for it.

Men began to drift into the place. They would come to the bar and order drinks. I kept easing down the bar toward its end because I didn't want to get boxed in so I couldn't get my gun out when I wanted it.

I didn't even notice Justin when he came in. Apparently the bartender told him I was waiting for him and that I'd said I was going to kill him, because I heard a shout that carried over the rest of the noise. "Where the hell's the kid that's goin' to kill me? Step out, kid, where I can get a look at you!"

I was down at the far end of the bar by then. I stepped out away from it, keeping the wall at my back. I had a moment when I wondered what I was doing here. Julesburg was the toughest town on the whole tough frontier and this saloon was probably one of the toughest places in town. I was a fool to think I could face men like these and live. I'd let Hackett talk me into this and because I had I was probably going to die on this dirty sawdust floor.

Down the room about halfway a man stepped away from the bar. He was a big man with a mustache something like the one Hackett had worn. He wore his gun a lot like I did, but the bottom of his holster was tied to his leg with a leather thong. I said, "I'm Jesse Hand. Ben Hackett sent me."

"Hackett?" He began to grin. "Oh yeah, Hackett." His grin widened. "Why didn't he come himself? Is something the matter with his hand? Or didn't he have the guts?"

I said, "He's dead." I'd been reluctant to come here for Hackett. I'd only done it because I figured I owed it to him. But suddenly I hated the man standing before me in that dimly lighted, smoke-filled room. I could picture him in my mind deliberately smashing Hackett's hand, probably grinning as he did.

I said, "Any time you're ready, Mr. Justin."

Nobody seemed to take me seriously. They were all grinning as Justin began to move toward me. I realized he didn't intend to shoot it out with me. He wanted to get close enough to get his hands on me. He probably intended to smash my hand the way he'd smashed Hackett's a long time ago.

I said, "You're not going to get close enough to put your hands on me. If you take another step I'm going to put a bullet in your leg."

I was nervous and a little scared by then and I guess he could hear it in my voice. He took another step.

I drew my gun the way I'd learned to draw it, and fired the instant it was clear. Justin's left leg buckled and he went down to the sawdust floor. There was surprise in his eyes, and shock, but there was something else. I knew that as soon as he got set he was going to draw.

I shoved my gun back in the holster and took a quick step to one side. Justin made his draw, awkwardly because he was on the floor. I waited until his gun was clear, then drew and shot him in the chest. His gun fired, but he was already dead. I didn't put my gun away. I stood there looking at the men, all of whose faces were turned toward me.

Nobody said anything and nobody acted like they were going to take it up. I began edging along the wall toward the door. I was almost to it when I heard a voice say, "I'll bet that's the kid them buffalo hunters was talkin' about. The one that killed three of them over an Indian."

I reached the door and backed through it into the street. I closed the door, turned and hurried away into the darkness. Behind me the door of the saloon opened and men streamed out. One man's voice carried clearly above the babble of indistinguishable voices, "Jesus Christ that kid is fast! I never saw anything so fast!"

I headed for the corral. I knew I had to get out of Julesburg quick. The buffalo hunters were here. Even if there wasn't any law in town, they'd be hunting me. And so would Sol Justin's friends.

I got my horses, mounted up and headed out of town. I decided right then that something had to change the way I was going or I was going to end up swinging at the end of a rope.

It was dark. I headed east because I'd made up my mind I was going back to Twin Forks and get Julia to marry me. I still had around fifty dollars in gold. I'd be able to work and I knew I'd be able to take care of myself and her. I wasn't afraid of her father anymore. I decided that after we were married we would go down to Texas and find Francisco Ross. He'd promised Hackett and me a job if we worked hard for him and I hadn't heard any complaints about the way we worked. I could put away my gun once we got to his ranch. We wouldn't have to worry about me causing any trouble for him there.

I rode steadily all night because I didn't know but what somebody would be chasing me. I'd been careful to give Justin a fair shake but I was thinking about the buffalo hunters, too.

It never occurred to me that I wasn't really giving a fair shake to anyone. I was faster and more accurate with my gun than anybody I'd come up against. Maybe Gus had been right when he said I was the fastest gun alive. Maybe nobody had a chance against me.

But I didn't really believe it. I guess I believed the saying that there never was a horse that couldn't be rode, nor a rider that couldn't be throwed. I just hadn't met up with anybody faster than me, so far. When I did, I'd be the one lying dead.

At dawn I stopped and gave my horse about an hour's rest. I didn't have any food and I hadn't passed any farms or settlements. Finally I killed a rabbit with my revolver when he jumped up ahead of my horse and streaked away.

I stopped long enough to build a fire out of buffalo chips and skin and cook the rabbit. Afterward, I went on again.

Nothing much happened to me during the ride back to Twin Forks. It took me two weeks of steady traveling. I avoided Abilene, although I did stop and buy supplies from one of the Texas Trail bosses who was holding his herd on the grass north of Abilene while he waited his turn to load. The Texas Trail hands eyed me and studied the way I wore my gun, but none of them challenged me.

I arrived in Twin Forks late at night. I went straight home. Grandpa got out of bed and let me in and he put his arms around me and hugged me as if I was still a little boy. We sat in the kitchen and talked for a couple of hours and I poured out the story of all the things that had happened to me. I didn't tell him about all the men I'd killed. I was ashamed even though I'd convinced myself every one of those killings was justified. But how would I have justified killing Sol Justin to grandpa?

Finally we went to bed after I'd told him I had come back for Julia. I could see he didn't approve, but he didn't say anything. In the morning we had breakfast. I put my gun away, saddled up my horse and rode over to Julia's house. I went up to the door and knocked. Julia's mother answered it and told me to go away. I said I didn't want to be disrespectful but I wanted to see Julia. She slammed the door but I stayed there and after a couple of minutes Julia opened it. I said, "I came back to ask you to marry me. They can't stop you if you say yes because you're sixteen."

She was white-faced and scared, but she nodded her head and said yes. I said, "I'll wait right here. You get what you need and tell your ma good-bye."

She went upstairs to get her things and her ma came and slammed the door in my face. I waited on the porch and after a while Julia came out. I helped her up on my horse and handed up her carpetbag. I led the horse to grandpa's. I didn't have but one saddle so I mounted Hackett's horse barebacked. Grandpa walked beside us and we rode over to the Methodist Church on Walnut Street. We'd dismounted and were just going into the church when I saw Mr. and Mrs. Delisa hurrying up the street. I told grandpa and Julia and the minister to go on inside and I stayed outside. Julia's father and mother were both pretty red in the face. Mr. Delisa looked like he was going to hit me the way he had once before.

I didn't have my gun on but I stood there facing him just as if I did. I could see it hanging from my saddlehorn out in the street. I ducked when he tried to hit me and keep out of reach. I said, "It ain't no use trying to do that to me, Mr. Delisa. I'm not going to hurt Julia. I'm just going to marry her."

"You lousy killer! You are like hell!"

I said, "You can't stop us, Mr. Delisa, and I'm not going to let you beat me up."

"How you going to stop me?"

"I guess I'll have to fight back."

Grandpa came out of the church. He said, "Delisa, you can't stop them. Julia's old enough."

Delisa said, "I'll kill him before I'll let him take her away."

"Isn't that what you say you've got against him? Killing?"

I don't know what Mr. Delisa might have done if Sheriff Coffey hadn't showed up just then. Coffey said Mr. Delisa would have to quiet down or he was going to throw him in jail for disturbing the peace. Mr. and Mrs. Delisa stamped away and I went into the church. The sheriff stayed outside.

Julia was crying but her determination to marry me hadn't weakened. The minister went through with the marriage ceremony and gave us a marriage certificate.

I told grandpa good-bye. There was considerable worry in his eyes as he shook my hand. It was as if he understood a lot more than I'd told him the night before. It was as if he was wondering if I wasn't going to end up the way my father had. I tried to tell him that I was worried about the same thing and that it was one reason I'd come home for Julia, but I couldn't make the words come out. We rode away and headed west and for half a day Julia was just silent and white and scared. I had put on the gun, though I wore it differently than I had before—higher, the way most other men, just average men, wore theirs.

I said, "We're going down to Texas, Julia, and I'm going to take good care of you. I've got a job waiting for me on a ranch and we're going to do just fine."

She tried to smile, but I could see she still was scared. I made up my mind she wasn't going to have to be scared for very long. And she wouldn't ever have to regret marrying me.

XII

JULIA WASN'T used to riding so we didn't travel very far each day. I didn't have much bedding, but we slept pretty close together, being just married, and kept warm that way. I didn't tell Julia that I'd killed seven men. As far as she knew, the two in Twin Forks were the only ones.

I told her we were going down to Texas to work on the ranch belonging to Francisco Ross. I bought an old saddle in the first town we passed through so that I wouldn't have to ride barebacked any more.

I guess I just didn't have enough sense to be afraid of traveling alone through the middle of Indian Territory and later through Comanche land. But I did have enough sense to travel by night and rest by day.

I'd thought I loved Julia before, but it was nothing compared to the way I grew to love her in the next few weeks. I knew I couldn't go on dragging her around the country though. She never complained about the hardships but I could see how hard it was for her to sleep when the ground was rocky or hard or when it rained.

And later, farther south, the heat grew unbearable. There weren't many ranches and no towns, so we were forced to live off the country. For days at a time we would eat only meat. Lots of times we didn't have enough water to more than wash it down.

I didn't know where Ross's ranch was and Texas is a mighty big place. I'd inquire at each ranch we came to, but none of the people I asked knew Francisco Ross.

Jobs seemed to be mighty scarce. Nobody was hiring hands, least of all green hands like myself. My money was almost gone and I knew I had to find work soon. For the first time in my life I began to get really scared.

We hit Fort Worth in late afternoon, dead broke and without anything to eat. I made camp at the edge of town in a thicket of mesquite. Julia looked white-faced and weak. I asked her if she was sick but she smiled and said, "No. I'm just a little tired. I'll be all right after I've had time to rest."

I said, "I'm going uptown and see if I can find some work. I'll bring back something to eat."

She nodded. "I wish I was more help. It seems like I'm just a worry to you."

I put my arms around her. My throat felt kind of tight. I was sorry I'd brought her away from her home in Twin Forks. I realized I'd brought her nothing but hardship. Now she was hungry too, and maybe sick. I said, "I'll be back as soon as I can."

I rode uptown. I asked at a dozen or more places for work but everybody I asked just shook their heads. I thought about Julia alone in that clump of mesquite. I couldn't face going back without a little food at least.

I was walking past a bank. Suddenly I stopped and stared at it. I crossed the street and looked into one of the windows.

It must have been past closing time, but the door was still unlocked. Through the window I could see some brass-barred cages. In one of them a man was counting piles of currency.

It suddenly seemed wrong that he should have so much and that Julia didn't even have anything to eat. I got off my horse and tied him to the rail. I went inside, pulling my bandanna up to cover my face as I did. I walked toward the window of the cage where the man was counting currency.

He was so absorbed that he didn't look up. I stood there for almost a minute, my hand on my gun, my bandanna covering the lower part of my face. And suddenly I realized what I was about to do. I realized that I was about to cross the line between living within the law and living outside of it, something I had never done before.

Quickly, I put up a hand and pulled the bandanna back where it belonged. I let my hand fall away from my gun. The man finished counting the pile of money and glanced up at me.

Something about my expression must have frightened him. His face lost color. He put a hand underneath the counter and I knew there was a gun down there. I said, "Mister, I need a job. I could sweep out or anything."

He shook his head, licking his lips. His hand stayed underneath the counter and his eyes stayed glued to my gun. I was afraid he was going to pull that gun out and I knew if he did I'd have to defend myself. I nodded. "Thanks. I just thought I'd ask." I turned and got outside as fast as I could.

I didn't look back. I untied my horse, mounted and rode down the street toward the livery barn. I was almost sick, thinking about what I'd nearly done. My hands shook and my stomach felt jumpy and upset.

When I reached the livery stable, I looked back toward the bank. The man who had been in the bank was running across the street toward the sheriff's office. He disappeared inside and I went into the livery barn.

He couldn't get me into trouble, I thought. He'd

never seen me with the bandanna up and I hadn't done anything but ask him for a job.

The stableman was skinny and wrinkled, with shrewd eyes that sized me up instantly. He knew I was broke and hungry and he knew I had to sell my horse. First I asked him for a job shoveling out stalls and when he refused, I said I wanted to sell my horse. While he was looking the horse over, I stepped to the door and glanced up the street.

The sheriff and the banker were crossing the street toward the bank together. It was almost dark. They went into the bank and I turned back to dicker with the stableman.

I was too tired and hungry to dicker much and he robbed me just as I had known he would. He gave me forty dollars for both horse and saddle, two double eagles. I walked out with them in my hand and with my saddlebags over my shoulder. I was thinking I'd bring Julia into town tonight and we'd eat at the hotel. Tomorrow we could buy some supplies and head out, riding double on Julia's horse.

From uptown, I heard a sound like a muffled shot, and for several moments I stood listening to see if there'd be a second one. There wasn't and I decided I had imagined it. The sheriff came out of the bank, only a shadowy figure now in the fading light, and went back across the street to his office. Hurrying, I headed for the mesquite thicket where Julia was.

She was lying on the ground, wrapped in all the blankets we had. Her face wasn't white any more. It was flushed. She didn't recognize me and she kept saying things that didn't make any sense. When I touched her, I discovered that she was burning up with fever.

She was going to have to have a real bed and some real good care. I could see that plain enough. She was in no shape to travel and I just had to go somewhere else and find a job. I was satisfied that there weren't any here.

I got Julia on her horse and wrapped her up with blankets. I headed back into Fort Worth leading the horse. It was now completely dark.

There had been low points in my life before, but I guess that night was the worst. I was scared to death Julia was going to die and I knew if she did I'd just as well die too. I didn't know where I'd get a job and I knew I had to have one because what I'd gotten for the horse wasn't going to last very long.

After I'd gone several blocks, I saw a woman walking along the street. I stopped her and said, "Ma'am, my wife is sick. Can you tell me where the nearest doctor is?"

She came close and looked up at Julia and she put up a hand and touched her cheek. Then she looked at me. She was a big, raw-boned woman and her voice was as harsh and raspy as any man's. She said, "Son, your wife's sick all right. You bring her along with me and I'll put her in bed. You can fetch the doctor whilst I'm doin' it."

She led the way to a big two-story frame house. I carried Julia in and the woman led me to an upstairs bedroom, carrying a lamp. I felt like an animal walking into her house. I was dirty and unshaven and I suddenly noticed for the first time that Julia wasn't much better off.

Her father had been right. I'd done her wrong in marrying her and taking her away from home. Now she was sick and might die in this lonesome, faraway place and it would be my fault if she did.

The woman shooed me out and I mounted and went after the doctor, following the directions she had given me. She said her name was Mrs. Ferguson and the doctor would know how to get to her house all right.

I found him without any trouble. While he was getting his things together I sat down at his desk and wrote Julia a note. I wasn't going to use up any of that forty dollars on myself when I knew she'd need it all before she was well again. I said in the note that I had to leave but that I'd be back as soon as I could. I asked the doctor for an envelope and I put the note in along with the two double eagles I'd gotten for the horse. I gave it to the doctor and said, "There's some money in there, along with a note for her. It'll take care of her until I can find me a job and send some more."

He asked, "Aren't you going back with me?" and I shook my head. I knew Julia was unconscious and out of her head and wouldn't know me anyway, maybe for days. If I saw her I'd stay and be using up money that she needed desperately.

He asked, "What kind of husband are you, anyway? She's sick. Do you think all she needs is money?"

I said, "Doctor, she's out of her head and likely will be for a long time. I ain't going to use up money that she might need before she's well. I got to find a job, and I've asked around in Fort Worth enough to know there just ain't no jobs here. You tell her I'll get word to her and that I'll be back just as soon as I can."

He looked at me kind of funny, but he didn't say any more. Maybe he'd never been broke and scared and maybe he didn't understand that I wasn't scared for me but for Julia. I'd always gotten by all right, but I had Julia now and that was different. I wasn't going to drag her around the country anymore like I'd been doing the past few weeks.

He took the envelope and put it into his bag and started walking in the direction of Mrs. Ferguson's house. I followed him and I waited until he'd been upstairs and had looked at Julia. When he came down, he said, "She's very ill. Very ill. But she couldn't be in better hands than Mrs. Ferguson's."

I thanked him and rode north out of town. I still

hadn't had anything to eat, but I didn't have any money to pay for food.

I figured I'd angle west at the first fork in the road and hope there were ranches that way where I could ask for work, and maybe get a meal even if there wasn't any work. I was riding along the dusty road at a trot when all of a sudden a bunch of men jumped out of a clump of mesquite ahead of me. The moon had come up and I could see them plain. They had rifles and shotguns and one of them yelled, "There's the murderin' sonofabitch!"

I hauled my horse to a halt and said, "Whoa! You got the wrong man. I haven't done anything "

"You're the one, all right. John Rafferty at the bank said who it was before he died."

For an instant I was stunned. Then I remembered the muffled shot I'd heard from down at the livery barn. I remembered seeing the sheriff come out of the bank shortly afterward. I couldn't believe it, but I had to believe it. These men weren't playing any joke.

Somebody had robbed the bank and killed the man who had been counting money inside of it. It seemed incredible but it couldn't have been anyone but the sheriff. He'd been inside when I'd heard the shot. When he'd come out, he hadn't been yelling the way a man would who has just discovered a robbery.

Rafferty wouldn't have said it was me when he knew that it was not. But the sheriff might have said he did, and that would be accepted by the townspeople as the gospel truth.

I was dead if I let them take me. I knew that instantly. Maybe they'd kill me if I ran, but it was a chance I had to take. I wheeled my horse to one side and spurred him toward the mesquite. Half a dozen guns roared behind me and several shot from one of the shotguns imbedded themselves in my back. They must have stung my horse too, because he ran as if the devil was after him.

Right then my gun was absolutely no good to me. I was fast with it, maybe the fastest, but that wasn't going to do me a damn bit of good if this posse caught up with me. I couldn't get them all and those who were left would just string me up to the nearest tree or to a wagon tongue if they couldn't find a tree.

They were pushing pretty hard and I had no choice but to push my horse hard enough to stay ahead of them. Looking back, I could see that they were beginning to string out as the fastest ones forged ahead and the slower ones fell behind.

I had some time to think after my first surprise began to fade away. Here I was, in the greatest danger of my life, and for something I hadn't done. But I couldn't fool myself. The gun had gotten me into it. The gun had scared the man at the bank and he'd told the sheriff he'd thought I intended to hold him up. It must have given the sheriff an idea. Rob the bank, kill Rafferty and blame it all on me.

There was a kind of sour irony in it. I thought of all the killing I'd done, the men in Twin Forks to save the life of Charlie Two Horses, McGinnis to recover my property and avenge the savage beating he'd given me, and all the others that I'd always been able to justify, however shakily.

Now I was going to pay the tab and for something I hadn't even done. I didn't see how I was going to get away this time. Too many men were after me, and their horses were fresher than mine.

I didn't know how to pray and maybe I wouldn't have prayed even if I had. I'd made promises to myself before, promises I hadn't kept. Maybe I had done so many bad things that I could never redeem myself. But I promised myself as I fled before that posse that if I got away, I would put away the gun for good. I'd get rid of it. I wouldn't ever carry a gun again.

I didn't keep that promise any more than I'd kept the ones I made before. Maybe the course of my life had been decided long before I was ever born.

XIII

RAFFERTY, THE banker who had been killed, must have been well-liked because the men in that posse stuck to me like glue. As soon as it got dark I changed directions to try and throw them off, but they must have had a real tracker along. I didn't fool them a bit. Trouble was, the grass was so long and the ground so soft that my horse left a plain trail galloping along, one that could be seen even by the faint light coming from the stars.

The posse was strung out by now for a mile or more. Only three men were close enough for me to worry about and they were falling steadily behind.

I figured their horses maybe weren't as tired as mine but they were livery stable horses not used to exercise. We came to some country that was broken and rocky and I slowed enough so that my horse didn't leave much of a trail traveling across the rocky ground. I went on this way for a while, then changed directions and rode for another half a mile. I could faintly hear them yelling to each other as I lined out straight north again. By the time they had figured out what I'd done and located my trail, I should be several miles ahead.

But I didn't fool myself. Throwing them off tonight wasn't going to do me any permanent good. They weren't going to quit. I had a long, hard ride ahead of me and I'd better keep my wits about me every minute of the time or I'd end up with a rope around my neck.

I began worrying about Julia. I realized that I might not know whether she had lived or died for months. I could write Mrs. Ferguson, and write Julia in her care, but I didn't dare give them a return address.

Along about two or three in the morning I

stopped to rest. I didn't have anything to eat but I drank some water that was strong with alkali.

I took off the saddle and fanned my horse with the saddle blanket and then rubbed him down real good. After that I gave him a full hour to rest, knowing it would pay me in the end. When I mounted and headed north again, he didn't act nearly as tired as he had before. I figured the posse men would be too anxious to rest their horses properly. They'd keep pushing, trying to catch up with me, and would end up with played-out horses that had to be destroyed.

But they had one big advantage over me. They knew the country and its inhabitants. They knew where they could get fresh horses while I did not.

I didn't bother trying to hide my trail anymore because I knew it would do no good. I just lined out straight north, watching my horse carefully and stopping him every once in a while to let him breathe and cool off a bit.

In midafternoon I saw a ranch ahead. It wasn't much of a ranch, just an adobe house dug back into a hill with a sod roof out of which weeds nearly three feet high had grown. There was an adobe corral and a windmill pumping water into a trough. There were three horses inside the corral.

I rode in. A man and a weatherbeaten woman came to the door. Three or four little kids peered at me from behind the woman's skirts. I said, "I'd just as well tell you the truth right off. I've got a posse after me because of a bank robbery and killing in Fort Worth. I didn't do it, but I don't expect you to believe that. I need a fresh horse and some grub. I haven't got a cent, but I give you my word I'll send you the money the first time I get any work."

The man started to shake his head so I said, "You do it, or I take what I want. It'll do you no good to tell me no. I don't want to hurt anybody but I'm desperate."

The woman said fearfully, "Give him the horse, Si. I'll put some things into a gunnysack."

The man reached down beside the door for his gun. I said, "You hadn't better. I've killed before and I can again."

He replaced the gun against the wall beside the door. He was a gaunt, sunbaked man, with eyes that seemed to be squinted permanently against the glare. His mouth was a thin, straight line. He still hadn't said a word. He came outside and I said, "Tell your missus not to make any trouble, mister. I don't want to hurt anyone but I will if you force me to."

He turned his head and called back toward the house: "Don't do nothing I don't tell you to!"

She didn't answer him and maybe it wasn't necessary. We walked to the corral and I followed, leading my worn-out horse. The man opened the corral gate and we went inside.

Two of the horses were old, sway-backed animals with harness galls on them. I supposed they'd been used for pulling a wagon, and maybe for pulling a garden plow. The other horse was a dappled gray, short and stocky, but sleek and strong. I asked, "How much for the trade?"

He looked at my horse. "That there's a pretty sorry-looking horse you got" he said, as if I had money in my hand.

I nodded. I didn't care how much he dickered or how much he wanted just so it wasn't more than I could pay. And I did intend to pay. He said, "I hate to part with that there gray. He's a mighty fine animal."

I said, "How much? Just don't get greedy. I can take him without paying you a dime."

He said, "Fifty dollars?"

I didn't want any arguments. It seemed like arguments always ended up with me killing somebody and I sure didn't want any more of that. I said, "You write down your name and the town where you get your mail." I unsaddled my horse and, when he caught the gray, threw the saddle on and cinched it down.

The woman came from the house carrying a gunnysack. I took it from her and looked inside to make sure she hadn't filled it with rocks. I was so hungry I wanted to reach in and grab something and stuff it into my mouth, but I didn't. I went over and filled my canteen at the windmill discharge pipe, then tied it and the gunnysack on behind the saddle. The man came out of the cabin with a scrap of paper and handed it to me.

I mounted. The woman was looking at me in a way that suddenly made me wonder what it would have been like to grow up with a mother and father like other kids. She said, "You ain't very old, son, to be out here all alone."

I wanted to turn the horse and go, but something held me still. I couldn't understand why the man hadn't made a fight out of it.

I said, "I'll send you the money. I give you my word."

Neither she nor her husband said anything more. She just kept looking at me with a kind of sadness in her eyes. It made me uneasy so I turned my horse and rode away. I swung around and looked back once to be sure nobody was going to take a shot at me with a rifle, but I needn't have worried about it. They were just standing there looking after me with their hands raised to shade their eyes against the sun. The kids were clustered beside the door, also looking after me. I don't suppose they saw a stranger more than once or twice a year so it was probably an event.

The posse men wouldn't get fresh horses at this place, I thought, unless they were willing to settle for those two sway-backed work horses. I suddenly felt safer than I had since I'd left Fort Worth.

But those little kids and the woman and the man had gotten me to thinking about Julia. We'd been married and together for several weeks. I began wondering if she was going to have a child.

Texas is a big country, stretching away for what looks like a thousand miles. A man can feel lonesomer in Texas than anyplace else in the world, I guess. I sure felt alone. I would have welcomed seeing Indians. I might even have welcomed seeing the posse coming on behind.

I wasn't fool enough to think I'd gotten clear away just because I hadn't seen the posse recently. I knew they'd keep going until they reached a telegraph. They'd send my description to towns all over the high plains. From now on I was going to have to be on my guard every moment of the time. I'd never know when someone would recognize me and begin shooting at me. There might even be a price on my head. Fortunately they had no photographs of me. All they had was my description and my name.

It was now late fall. I got caught in a norther howling out of the high country in Colorado, and for two days huddled in the lee of a cutbank wondering if I was going to freeze to death.

I had a lot of time to think while I huddled there, about where my life was going. It looked like I was heading straight for prison or a scaffold. But there had to be some way to change. There had to be something I could do to earn a living for myself and maybe later for Julia. There had to be a way to live without fighting and killing and living by the gun.

If I'd only been able to find the ranch of

Francisco Ross, I thought. Then I wouldn't have gone to Fort Worth and I wouldn't have this posse after me.

The norther finally stopped blowing and, half-frozen, I mounted and continued north. On the bank of the Red River I came on a trading post run by a man named Beauchamp. I stayed there overnight and went on in the morning without having been able to buy either grub for myself or oats for my horse.

Living off the country, traveling mostly by night to avoid discovery by Indians, I continued north, now bearing toward the west. I struck the Arkansas and followed it, detouring around Fort Lyons and going on into Pueblo.

I took off my gun at the outskirts of town and put it into my saddlebags. But as I rode through the adobe Mexican section of the town, I realized how foolish it would be to get caught without my gun. By now there most certainly were wanted posters on me in every lawman's office for a radius of five hundred miles. To get caught without my gun would be suicide.

I got it out of the saddlebags and put it on again. I reached the business section and dismounted before the first saloon. I'd found a dime in my saddlebags when I got my gun back out. It was the price of a couple of beers, and I could eat from the free lunch counter while I was drinking them. After that, maybe something would turn up.

The place was nearly deserted. There was a Mexican tending bar. He was talking to another Mexican who stood at the far end of it. A couple of bearded men were playing cards at a table against the wall.

I stepped up to the bar next to the free lunch and ordered beer. The bartender slid it down to me and I put down my dime. I got a plate and began to fill it. When I figured I had enough, I picked up the plate, the beer and my nickel change and walked to a table over against the wall. I sat down facing the door and the bar, with the wall at my back.

My prospects looked mighty bleak. Jobs were hard to find and I didn't dare take off my gun, so most jobs would not be available to me. You can't work in a store wearing a low-slung gun.

A man came in. He was different than the others in the place. His range clothes were dusty and worn and he wore a sheepskin coat. He had a broad-brimmed hat and spurs on the heels of his boots. He glanced quickly at me once, then, after he'd been served, turned and looked steadily at me. I stared back, wondering if he was a lawman or bounty hunter who had recognized me from the description that was probably circulating.

He seemed particularly interested in the way I wore my gun. At last he picked up his glass and bottle and crossed the room to me. I shifted position slightly so my gun would be instantly available.

The man stopped and looked down at me. He had the bottle in one hand the glass in the other. He said, "Mind if I sit down?"

I shook my head. "I don't mind, but I don't know you and you don't know me."

He said bluntly, "On the dodge, aren't you?"

I began to feel angry. I said irritably, "What makes you think so?"

He shrugged. "Maybe I was wrong. It don't matter to me anyhow."

"What does matter? What do you want?"

"I figured maybe you might need a job, that's all. I got a look at your horse out front. He's been traveling a long time and he's thin. You look a little trailworn yourself."

I asked, "What kind of a job?"

"Ranch job."

I said, "I'm no cowman. I helped on a trail drive once for a month or so but that was all."

"How good are you with that gun of yours?"

"Good enough. I can take care of myself."

He said, "Fifty a month and keep."

"What do I have to do?"

"What I tell you to."

"Fifty a month is too much for ordinary cowhands. You can hire for less than that."

He said, "I need men who know how to use their guns. I need men that will discourage the rustling that's going on."

It sounded reasonable so I nodded. I said. "I want

121

an advance. I want the first two months' pay right now."

He studied me carefully for a long, long time. At last he took out a roll of bills and peeled off five twenties. He handed them to me. He said, "I'm Jason Kraft. My place is the K Quarter Circle on Andy Creek northeast of here. You figuring to get drunk on that money, son?"

"I'm going to send half of it to my wife and half of it to a man I owe. I'll be ready to go as soon as you are."

He was looking at me strangely. He finally nodded and stood up. "Be back here in half an hour then."

I wondered how he knew that I'd come back. He didn't, I supposed. But he probably figured he could make me regret it if I didn't show.

I knew exactly why he was hiring me. He wanted me to scare somebody with my gun. He'd seen the way I wore it and he'd sized me up by my horse, my clothes and by the look of me.

I went out. I went to a mercantile store and got some paper, envelopes, and a pencil. I changed one of the twenties Kraft had given me. I wrote to Julia telling her I was sorry I'd had to leave so suddenly and told her I hadn't done what they said I had. I said I hoped she was all right now and I told her I loved her but that she'd better go back to Twin Forks as soon as she was well enough. I put forty-five dollars of the money in and sealed the envelope. I put fifty into another envelope, sealed it and addressed it to the man where I'd gotten the gray horse.

I went out into the street. There was a stage station across the street from the hotel. I asked the stage driver where it was going and he said Denver. I gave him both envelopes and a dollar and asked him to mail them for me when he arrived. He said he would.

I got on my horse and rode back to the saloon where I'd met Jason Kraft. He was waiting for me. We rode toward the edge of town.

He asked, "What name do you go by?"

I started to tell him Jesse Hand, but I stopped before the words were out. I said, "Jones. Russ Jones." He said, "All right, Russ Jones. As far as I'm concerned, the past is past. All I want is to hold my land and keep my cattle from being stolen. Your job is to help. If you do your job we'll get along just fine."

XIV

JASON KRAFT'S ranch on Andy Creek was a good twelve or thirteen miles from town. It was dark long before we got to it. Mostly we rode without saying anything. I didn't have anything to say to Jason Kraft and I guess he didn't have anything to say to me. For the first time I had hired out my gun.

There were still some lights burning when we

rode in. Kraft dismounted beside the corral and turned his horse into it. He waited until I had followed suit, then pointed to a log building across the yard in which a single lamp still burned. "There's the bunkhouse. I'll see you in the morning."

I picked up my saddle and crossed to the bunkhouse. Carrying it I went inside. I put it down just inside the door.

There were maybe a dozen bunks in the bunkhouse. Kraft must have a pretty good-sized ranch, I thought, to need that many men. Three men were playing poker at a table in the middle of the room. The lamp sat on one corner of the table. All three of them looked up at me. I could hear someone snoring in one of the bunks.

I said, "I'm Russ Jones. Mr. Kraft hired me in town today."

The three continued to look at me, paying particular attention to the way I wore my gun. I stepped closer to the table. I was about to ask which bunk I should take when one of the men said, "Russ Jones hell! You're Jesse Hand. I seen you kill Sol Justin over in Julesburg last summer."

I said, "I'm Russ Jones, if you don't mind."

The man said, "Sure. I don't know why I should mind."

I asked, "Which bunk should I take?"

He pointed one out. I went to my saddle and untied my blanket roll. I crossed to the bunk and spread my blankets out on it.

I withdrew my gun from its holster and laid it on the bunk where my hand could rest on it. I took off my clothes, crawled in and pulled the blankets up over me. I could hear other men breathing now. One had begun to snore. The quiet slap of the cards went on and I heard the clink of money occasionally. Once in a while one of the poker players would utter a quiet curse.

I had a job at least, I thought. I had been recognized but maybe the fact that I was wanted for murder and bank robbery wouldn't follow me to this ranch for quite a while.

I made up my mind on one thing. I was going to do more than hunt rustlers and scare Kraft's neighbors while I was here. I was going to learn cattle work. I was going to become a cowhand so that when I left I could get a job doing only that. I wanted to be able to hold a job that did not depend on my skill with a gun.

Then, if I worked hard and stayed out of trouble and changed my appearance and my name, I might sometime be able to get Julia to come to me. We could lose ourselves in this empty country where nobody who had known Jesse Hand would ever find us again. Maybe eventually I'd be able to live down the things that had happened since I first left home.

It took me a long time to go to sleep. I kept thinking how much had happened in less than a year. It had all started in April and it was only

November now. I realized that my birthday had passed unnoticed nearly a month ago. I was eighteen now.

Eight men were dead by my hand since that morning when the two strangers rode into Twin Forks and started tormenting Charlie Two Horses. Thinking about that, I finally slipped into an uneasy sleep.

It was snowing hard in the morning when we woke up. A cold wind was blowing down out of the north. We trooped up to the house for breakfast before it was even light.

The house was an enormous, two-story frame building painted a bright barn red. The kitchen alone was as big as most houses and had a long table with benches on either side that would seat thirty or forty men. There was a Chinese cook and a big Negro woman helping him. Jason Kraft was there, sipping coffee beside the stove.

A wide double doorway led into the living room. Looking through I saw there wasn't any furniture. The room was filled with supplies, with barrels of flour and sugar, rolls of barbed wire, kegs of nails, lumber, sacks of oats and barley. A passageway led through the stacked-up supplies to a wide stairway. I supposed Kraft and the Chinese cook and the Negro woman slept upstairs.

Breakfast consisted of fried side meat, flapjacks and sorghum, fried potatoes, corn bread, oatmeal and coffee. I hadn't seen a spread like that for weeks. I ate like the meal was going to be my last.

After eating, everybody lighted up cigars or pipes, or rolled wheat-straw cigarettes. I'd never started smoking so I didn't now. Kraft called off several names and sent the men whose names he called out on various jobs of cattle work. After they had left, four men remained, including me. The other three were older but we all had one thing in common. We'd been hired for our guns, not our cattle savvy or ranch experience.

Kraft said, "Russ Jones is the new man here. He's young, but he says he can take care of himself. Russ, meet Leon Alvarez, Nate Purdue and Tom Strang."

I shook hands all around. Purdue was the one who had recognized me in the bunkhouse the night before. He said, "I've seen this boy work. Over in Julesburg last summer. He's good."

It felt nice to have him say that. Kraft said, "I figure this snow is going to let up around noon. When it does, there's going to be a lot of tracks. If we start now, we can be over there on Horse Creek when it stops."

Nobody made any comment. We got up and headed for the door. As I reached it, Kraft said, "Get yourself a fresh horse, Jones. We've got a hard ride ahead of us. You got a coat?"

I shook my head. He said, "There's a pile of 'em in the other room. Pick out one you like."

I went into the other room. It looked like there

was enough stuff in here to keep the ranch operating independently for months. I found the pile of coats and picked out a warm sheepskin that fitted me. I also found a pair of gloves. Neither was new but they were good enough.

I went out. With a warm coat and gloves, the blowing snow and cold didn't bother me. I got my saddle out of the bunkhouse and carried it to the corral.

The regular cowhands were just now riding away to their various tasks. I wasn't much of a roper but I managed to drop a loop onto a tough, shaggy sorrel without looking too green. I bridled and saddled him and led him out of the corral. I knew he'd buck and while I was no bronc rider, I figured I could stay on his back.

He bucked all right and I stayed with him but when I got tired of it I yanked his head up and made him stop. Nobody was paying any attention to me. Kraft came out and caught up a horse and the five of us rode out toward the north, right into the howling wind and blowing snow. The horses didn't like it much but we forced them to keep their heads into the wind.

It sure didn't look like the storm was going to let up. I'd have bet a month's pay it wouldn't, but sure enough, along in late morning the snow slowed and finally stopped. The sky got lighter and at last the sun showed as a bright spot nearly overhead.

The country was a lot like Kansas. It was rolling

country, with sometimes a rocky rim guarding a low plateau, or a wide, sandy, dry stream bed, or a dry wash slashing across the level plain. The vegetation was buffalo grass which is a short clump grass with burly blades. It sends up a stem with seed pods on it. It's pretty sorry-looking stuff for anyone used to the lush grass that grows where it rains a lot, but it sure can put fat on a cow. There was sagebrush, too, and yucca and prickly pear, and there were occasional clumps of another kind of cactus I couldn't name.

Now and then we would see little bunches of cattle, dark spots against the expanse of white. Mostly they were Texas cattle, but I saw a few red-and-white Hereford bulls. The calves showed the bulls' influence. Eventually, I thought, Kraft was going to have his herd bred up to where it amounted to something. Anybody could see how much better Hereford cattle would be for beef than those stringy Texas cattle. But the new strain would probably retain the toughness and foraging ability of the Texas breed.

Kraft said, "There's a family named Suggs that lives over here on Horse Creek. They've got a deal going with a crooked slaughterhouse in Leadville. They always try to pull out of here with a bunch during a snowstorm so they can't be trailed."

I asked, "How did you know the storm was going to quit?"

He grinned. "I didn't know. I just felt it. But if we're lucky today, we ought to catch them with the goods."

I didn't ask what would happen if we did catch them driving his cattle toward Leadville, which was over in the high mountains to the west. I supposed he'd take them to Pueblo and turn them over to the law unless they put up a fight. I figured he had us four along in case they did.

We struck a drainage that Kraft said was Horse Creek and followed it north. We'd gone about half a dozen miles when we suddenly struck a trail. Kraft got off his horse and studied the trail for quite a while, casting back and forth and walking ahead for maybe an eighth of a mile. When he got back on his horse he said, "It's them all right. They've got eleven head as near as I can tell."

Eleven head didn't sound like much, but at twenty-five dollars a head it added up to two hundred and seventy-five dollars. More than five months' wages for a gunhand. Nearly ten months' wages for an ordinary cowhand. Maybe more than the Suggs family could make honestly in half a year.

It was a long drive to Leadville. I'd have guessed it was around a hundred miles. If they stayed away from well-traveled roads, it would probably take them a couple of weeks to drive the cattle there.

I asked, "How many times a year do you figure they do this, Mr. Kraft?"

"They've been getting two hundred head a year from me as near as I can tell. I've tried getting the law to help me out, but they say they've got to have evidence. I finally decided I'd just take care of it myself."

My stomach felt a little emptier when he said that. But I'd hired on for my gun and I'd taken a hundred dollars from him. I had expected trouble when he hired me.

It wasn't that I was afraid. But if I was going to find a way to live without killing, this wasn't it. Still, I had to live some way. If I stayed here on Kraft's ranch, at least I'd be learning the cattle business.

We slogged on through snow that was about six inches deep. The trail was plain enough and easily followed. We reached the Suggs ranch and rode into the yard.

The house was built out of railroad ties that I supposed the Suggs family had stolen from the railroad. Between the ties, it was chinked with mud. A plume of smoke came from the tin chimney on the roof. Half a dozen dogs began to bark at us and a woman came to the door, a shotgun in her hands.

She was a thin, tired-looking, middle-aged woman who looked as if she'd had about all the trouble she could take. I figured it wouldn't take very much to make her pull the trigger of that scattergun. Kraft asked, "Your menfolks home, Mrs. Suggs?"

"You know they ain't. You been trailin' 'em, ain't you?"

"We've been trailing them."

"What you going to do when you catch up to 'em?"

Kraft said, "I guess that depends on them."

She nodded, a kind of dumb helplessness in her face. Kraft turned his horse and rode away. The woman stared after us.

We picked up the trail again and followed it. About a mile from the home place it turned due west, now cutting across low hills and ridges as it headed for the mountains.

Kraft kept his horse at a steady trot, a gait not very easy on a man but one a horse can maintain all day. The trail seemed fresher all the time and I knew we were gaining on the rustlers. Some of the cattle droppings looked as if they were scarcely cold.

At last we topped a long ridge and caught a glimpse of them going over the next ridge west. Kraft halted us until they were out of sight.

From the ridge-top he stared at the country, frowning as he did. He turned his head and said, "We could play this cute, I suppose, but I'm damned if I see any sense in it. We'd just as well go on and overtake them from the rear. They're less likely to go for their guns if they've had time to think it out than if they've been surprised."

That made sense to me. I was beginning to like

Jason Kraft. He had apparently tried to obtain justice from the law. Even now, he didn't want any shooting if he could avoid it. But he wanted his cattle back. And he wanted the rustling to stop.

XV

FOUR MEN were driving the stolen bunch. One was close to Jason Kraft's age, although he looked a lot older when we got close to him. The other three must have been his sons. The youngest was about my age and the oldest looked to be nearly thirty.

They had seen us coming while we were still a quarter-mile away. I had thought they were going to bolt but they did not. They halted and turned their horses to face us. The cattle went on a little ways and also stopped. They stood, dumbly waiting in the snow.

We were five to four and except for Kraft, all of us were gunhands. I unbuttoned my sheepskin and tucked back the flap on the right side so that I could get at my gun. I took the glove off my right hand. The others were also preparing themselves and the Suggs men couldn't have failed to see.

The old man had a rifle in the saddle boot. I couldn't tell whether his sons were armed or not. If they did have guns, they were hidden beneath their coats.

Once we got them within the range of our revolvers, Kraft called, "Shuck your guns, boys.

Drop 'em nice and easy and nobody will get hurt."

Old man Suggs' face was kind of gray. His eyes had a trapped look to them. He ran his tongue over his lips nervously.

His sons weren't scared. They were defiant. The old man said, "Easy boys. Do what he says."

They looked at him as if they had expected more than this from him. He said, "I guess I always knew this day would come. What are you going to do with us, Mr. Kraft?"

One of the sons said, "Don't call the sonofabitch Mister, pa. He—"

Kraft said, "What I do depends on you."

The oldest of the sons said bitterly, "Sure, what you do depends on us. We got a hell of a fine choice, ain't we? If we give up you take us to Pueblo and we each get two years in the pen. Or you hang us one by one. If we put up a fight we get gunned down here an' now by them fancy gun-slicks you got with you."

Kraft said, "Frank, you should have thought of all that before you started helping yourself to my steers."

Frank Suggs suddenly whirled his horse and sank his spurs. The startled animal bolted. Beside me a gun barked and Suggs flopped sideways out of the saddle. His foot caught in the stirrup but the terrified horse didn't stop. He galloped away, with Frank Suggs's body dragging helplessly.

The other sons grabbed frantically for their guns.

The father yanked his rifle from the boot and levered in a shell.

I reacted instinctively. I felt my gun in my hand and my thumb on the hammer. The gun came up, leveled and fired instantly.

There was no need to fire a second time. Mr. Suggs dropped the rifle and as he did, his horse began to buck. He sailed limply out of the saddle and landed in the snow. He didn't move. There was no blood because of his heavy coat but I knew where he'd been hit. I also knew that he was dead.

The two boys were also dead, riddled by bullets from the guns of Alvarez, Purdue and Strang. Kraft had not drawn his gun.

Kraft's face was bloodless as he stared at the bodies in the snow. Frank's body had come loose from the stirrup and now lay a couple of hundred yards away. His horse had joined the others. They stood in a group beyond the bunched cattle, reins dragging in the snow.

Kraft said, "Jesus! I didn't want this to happen! Why didn't they just give up?"

Purdue asked without feeling, "What you want to do with them, Mr. Kraft? Leave 'em, or load 'em up an' take 'em home?"

Kraft didn't seem able to make up his mind. I said, "You can't take them to that woman, Mr. Kraft. If you do, we'll have to kill her too."

He said, "Load 'em up. We'll take them in to the

undertaker in Pueblo. I have to notify the sheriff anyway."

I stared at him uneasily. If he was going to take the bodies in to Pueblo and make a report to the sheriff, it would mean that I'd have to testify at a coroner's inquest. If the coroner ruled that we should be tried, then my real name would inevitably come out. When it did I'd be arrested and tried for the bank robbery and killing I was accused of in Fort Worth.

Purdue rode over and caught up the horses that had belonged to the Suggs men, one by one. He led them back to where the bodies were. He dismounted. Strang and Alvarez had also dismounted and were now preparing to load the bodies. Kraft remained on his horse and so did I.

I said, "Mr. Kraft, I didn't give you my right name. I'm wanted in Fort Worth and even if it's for something I didn't do, I can't afford to go to Pueblo with you."

He looked at me. There was no sympathy in his eyes, only something that looked like distaste. He asked, "Then what do you want to do?"

"I wanted to stay and work for you. I wanted to learn the cattle business. Now I guess I can't take the chance. I can't pay back the hundred dollars you gave me, though. Not now at least."

He said, "No need to pay it back. You earned it." There was a kind of bitterness in his voice, as though he regretted everything that had happened here. I didn't understand that. He'd hired gun-fighters so that he could stop the rustling. He'd stopped it. Now he seemed to be sorry that he had.

I said, "If it's all right about the money, I guess I'll be going then."

He nodded but he didn't look at me. I turned my horse and rode away, without even looking back.

Something was eating at my insides as I rode across the snowy plain, heading God knew where. I was a killer now. Besides being an outlaw and robber, I had become a man who killed for pay. I'd never seen Mr. Suggs in my life before. I'd had nothing against the man. A hundred dollars had been the price of his life. Kraft had said as much when he said I'd earned my pay.

I could tell myself it had been self-defense, but it was a lie and I knew it was a lie. I had hired out my gun. For fifty dollars a month I had agreed to kill whoever Jason Kraft wanted killed. That was the honest-to-God truth and all the lying in the world wasn't going to change it one damn bit.

My chest felt cold and my stomach felt hollow and empty. How in the hell was I going to change? How was I going to learn to make an honest living without always turning to the gun? How could I ever expect to see Julia again if I did not?

Down deep I suppose I knew the answer even then. I could take off the gun and throw it down into the snow. I could ride away from it. I could forget how to use it and never handle a gun again.

But I didn't have the courage for that. Maybe I still liked to think of myself as the fastest gun alive. I was, after all, only eighteen years old. My gun made me powerful and power is a very heady wine.

I headed west into the mountains because I knew that would be the best place to lose myself until the business in Fort Worth had blown over and been forgotten.

At that time, Leadville was a booming community. There were a lot of tents and hastily erected shacks as well as a few permanent-looking log buildings, both cabins and stores. I had a choice of working in one of the mines or for some placer claim operator, or of working for one of the saloonkeepers as a guard. Each of the saloons handled a lot of gold every day and the law was pretty weak, what little there was of it.

I took a job working for an Irishman named Jake Flanigan in a saloon called the Nugget. I had the night shift, from noon to midnight. All I had to do was be on hand.

It was a tiresome job, with nothing much to do but stand or sit around. I didn't smoke and I didn't drink. There was a period in early afternoon when there weren't more than a handful of miners in the place and not much to keep the gamblers occupied, so one of them, who called himself Lucky LaRue, offered to teach me a few things about the trade.

Until then I'd thought gambling was honest, but I sure found out different from LaRue. He started out slowly with me, in much the same way Hackett had taught me how to use a gun. First I was to learn to handle the cards, to get familiar with them. I sat at a table for days, doing nothing but shuffle cards. LaRue said that anyone as good with a gun as me ought to be a natural with cards. It was in the hands, he said. When he thought I was good enough he began to show me a few gambler's tricks. I also practiced these for days, but not in the open where somebody might see. After several weeks of practice in handling cards, in dealing off the top or bottom at will, or even out of the middle of the deck, LaRue undertook to teach me the games themselves. Poker was the one most men preferred, he said, so he taught me poker, the odds, the way to bluff when your opponent was playing scared, the way to seem to have one thing when actually you had something entirely different in your hand. There were plenty of ways to win at poker honestly, he said, and a man was a fool who played dishonestly when it wasn't necessary. The only time to employ the tricks, he said, was when you had your back against the wall and had to win.

It was a savage winter in the Colorado mountains, more savage in Leadville than elsewhere because of the altitude. Snow was sometimes drifted ten or fifteen feet deep in spots. The streams froze solid so that none of the placer claims were being worked. Some of the underground mines continued to operate, but there were plenty of idle men around all the time.

It was a paradise for gamblers, and for the saloonkeepers too. I gave up my job with Flanigan in favor of gambling. He didn't need me any longer since all the roads were closed and nobody could get in or out anyway.

I discovered that gambling beat living by the gun. It paid better. I remembered what LaRue had taught me, particularly the part about not playing dishonestly unless it was necessary. By the first of May I had five hundred dollars in a sack in Flanigan's big safe.

During the winter I killed three men. And by May I enjoyed a reputation in Leadville too. They had seen me draw and shoot three times. The stories about how fast I was grew with each retelling until by spring my hand was as fast as a snake's darting tongue.

I had now killed twelve men in all, and killing had become an accepted thing with me. Wherever I went, I killed. Two of the three I'd killed during the winter had accused me of cheating them. One of the two had been right, the other wrong. The third I had killed because he tried to hold up the game I was playing in.

It wasn't hard to justify what I had done. Justification seemed to come easier each time. I didn't have much more trouble justifying my killing of the man I had cheated than I had justifying my killing of the one that I had not.

When the roads opened in the spring, I withdrew my sack of gold from Flanigan's safe, mounted my horse and headed east. I knew I had to see Julia once more. I had to know if she was all right, and if she was going to bear my child. I had to hold her in my arms once more.

I followed the Arkansas River which has its source on the spine of the Continental Divide. I went through Pueblo at night, without stopping except for supplies. I didn't know whether the law would be looking for me for killing Mr. Suggs or not but I didn't see any use taking chances I didn't have to take.

I stopped in Abilene and stayed several days to give my horse a rest. The first of the herds had already arrived and a second arrived while I was there. There were famous men in Abilene that year. Wild Bill Hickok was there, and John Wesley Hardin, and Ben and Billy Thompson and Phil Coe.

All of them seemed to have heard of me. They were pleasant and friendly and respectful toward me. Wild Bill Hickok had been appointed town marshal earlier. He made his headquarters in the Alamo Saloon so that he could supplement his marshal's salary with gambling winnings. He did not, apparently, keep a file of wanted posters. He considered his job to be keeping the peace in Abilene and nothing else. What anybody had done outside of Abilene was none of his concern.

I spent most of my time sitting in on a game in the Alamo. The third day I was in town I was sitting there playing poker with four men. Hickok was at another table. It was about four in the afternoon. The doors banged open and a young man about my age walked in.

He was dressed like a cowhand, so he had probably come up the trail. He looked at Hickok and then he looked at me. He crossed to where I was. "You Jesse Hand?"

I nodded, a little surprised that he would know my name when I'd never seen him before in my life.

He said, "I hear you're fast as a rattlesnake." He glanced at Hickok as he said that.

I didn't say anything. I just waited for him to say whatever it was he had come to say. He didn't waste time. "I also hear you're as yellow-bellied as a damned horned toad. I hear you shot all the men you've killed in the back."

The four men playing with me suddenly lost interest in the game. They scattered like quail. The man looked over toward Hickok. He said, "Stay out of this, marshal. It'll be a fair fight."

Hickok didn't move. He only said, "Take my advice and get out of here while you're still alive."

"Huh uh. I'm going to see how fast this Jesse Hand really is."

I shoved back my chair. I made it a practice not to sit so I couldn't get at my gun, but the table was in the way and while I could shoot through it in a pinch, the wood might deflect the bullet and make me miss. I said, "Mind telling me your name?"

"It's Billy Coats. I'm up from Fort Worth. You're worth a thou—"

I didn't see any sense in letting him spill what he knew about me being wanted in Fort Worth. I said quickly, "If you're going to draw, why don't you draw and get it over with? You're spoiling my poker game. That is, if you've got the guts to back up your big mouth with your gun."

I sat there as coldly as an executioner waiting for him to draw. I knew I could beat him.

I saw his eyes narrow slightly as his brain willed his hand to move. I began my draw instantly.

He was fast but he wasn't nearly fast enough. His gun had cleared but had not leveled when my bullet smashed into him. His right arm dangled for an instant before the gun slipped out of his hand. He took several steps backward and then sat down. He stared at me. He seemed to be trying to say something.

I knew what it was. I also knew I'd better shut him up before he let everybody here know I was wanted for murder and bank robbery in Fort Worth and that there was a thousand-dollar reward for me dead or alive. I fired and the bullet knocked him over from his sitting position. He didn't move again.

I was still sitting down. I punched out the empties, then took two cartridges out of my gunbelt and reloaded my gun. I shoved it into the holster. I glanced at Hickok, then at the men I'd been playing poker with. I said, "Let's get back to the game."

They stared at me as if I was some kind of animal. I could see that they were scared of me. They came and picked up their money but they left the pot behind. They all went out the door as quickly as they could. I gathered up the pot. Someone had sent for the undertaker, but he had not yet arrived. I looked at Hickok. "Fair fight, wasn't it?"

He nodded without saying anything.

I went out and walked toward the hotel.

XVI

I LEFT Abilene in a vicious mood. I was angry at the men I'd been playing poker with. Where the hell did they get off, looking at me the way they had? I hadn't picked a fight with that damned kid. He'd picked one with me. He'd come into the Alamo to kill me and he sure had tried. It wasn't my fault that I beat him to the draw.

And Hickok. Where did he get off giving me that look as if he thought I was an executioner?

I rode east, pushing my horse a lot harder than was necessary. It was as if Twin Forks and Julia, if she was there, were drawing me the way the prospect of water will draw a man who is dying of thirst. But what I was really seeking was neither Julia nor Twin Forks. It was salvation. I suppose I thought that if I could just get back home where it all began, maybe I could pretend none of it had ever happened at all.

I came into Twin Forks pretty late. It was two or three in the morning, I suppose. I didn't look at my watch. It was too dark to see the hands and it didn't seem important enough to strike a match.

I went straight to grandpa's house. I went around to the back and tied my horse to a tree. I went in without knocking and closed the kitchen door. I don't know why I took those precautions. Instinct, I suppose.

Once inside the kitchen with the door closed behind me, I called, "Grandpa! You here? It's Jesse."

I heard the bed creak upstairs, and almost immediately afterward heard the creaking floorboards as grandpa crossed the room and started down the stairs. He came into the kitchen in darkness and he didn't light a lamp. That puzzled me.

His voice was different than it had ever been before. He said coldly, "What do you want?"

"What do I want? What's the matter with you? This is Jesse and I've come home."

"This ain't your home. Not anymore."

I knew then that he'd heard about the bank robbery and killing in Fort Worth. I said, "Julia's home. That's it, isn't it? And she told you about me being accused of that killing and bank robbery."

He interrupted, "Julia didn't tell anything. She's loyal to you though I'm damned if I know why. A couple of Pinkerton men followed her from Fort Worth. They're still in town, waiting for you to show."

"Aren't you going to ask the whether I did it or not?"

"I don't have to. You did it all right. And a lot of other things You're a mad dog, Jesse. You're a mad dog who likes the taste of blood."

I took a step toward him, angry because he was so ready to condemn.

He didn't flinch. He made a vague shape in the dark kitchen, his white nightshirt standing out plainly in spite of the fact that there wasn't any light. He asked, "How many is it now, Jesse? Ten? Twelve? And how many more will you kill before you die?"

I said, "Damn you—"

"That's right, Jesse. Cuss me out. Maybe if I crowd you enough you'll shoot me like you shot all them other men."

"I never shot anybody that wasn't trying to shoot me."

"How about the bank teller, Jesse?"

"I didn't shoot him. And I didn't rob the bank. All I did was ask him for a job. I don't know what happened afterward."

Grandpa didn't seem to have heard. He said, "Get out of here, Jesse. Leave Twin Forks tonight. I'll do this much for you. I won't tell the Pinkerton men that you were here."

I stared at him, glad he couldn't see my face. I was mad and I knew it showed. I'd been turned out of my own home. I was being sent away by one of the only two blood relatives I had in the world.

I asked, "Is Julia all right?"

"She's all right. She had lung fever down in Fort Worth but that Mrs. Ferguson got her over it."

"I've got to see her before I go."

"Like hell! You get out of town without bothering her or I'll put the sheriff and those two Pinkerton men on you! I swear it, Jesse. I'll turn you in myself!"

"I guess you'll have to, then. Because I'm going to see Julia."

He lunged across the room, a white shadow in that baggy nightshirt. I guess he was after a rifle and I reacted instinctively. My gun was in my hand and the hammer coming back before I even realized it.

I eased the hammer down and returned the gun to its holster, hoping he hadn't seen. But he had. He said bitterly, "It's instinct now, isn't it Jesse? Kill. That's all you know anymore."

I said, "Damn it, grandpa, stop pushing me. I've been forced into things."

He had a rifle in his hands. I heard the hammer

147

cock. He said, "I'm not going to let you go see Julia."

I turned my back on him. "You can't stop me because you haven't got what it takes to shoot. I'm going over there right now. If you think you have to turn me in, then you'd better get at it."

I crossed the kitchen and went out the door. I half-believed grandpa would really shoot and I suppose that proved as much as anything how far down the road I'd gone. He slammed the door behind me so hard it rattled the windowpanes.

I untied my horse and mounted. It wasn't likely that the Pinkerton men were watching this late at night, but I didn't take any chances. I rode along the backstreets until I came to Julia's house. I wasn't sure how I was going to rouse her without rousing her folks as well. But I did know that if I woke either her father or mother they'd make such an uproar that the whole damn town might be aroused.

I tied my horse to a fence a couple of houses down the street and went on afoot. I'd have to take the chance that Julia still slept in the same bedroom. I went around to the back of the house. I'd picked up some small stones, and as soon as I was in position, I tossed one carefully at Julia's window. It struck the glass with a sound that was loud enough to wake everyone in the neighborhood. Or at least that was the way it seemed to me.

Almost right away, I saw something white

moving behind the window. I tossed another stone, letting this one rattle on the roof.

The window raised. A woman was leaning out but I couldn't tell whether it was Julia or not. I called, "Julia?"

Her voice was breathless, unbelieving. "Jesse!"

I said, "It's me. Climb out the window onto the roof. If you jump I'll catch you."

She climbed out the window and in bare feet and nightgown crept to the edge of the porch roof. I said, "Now. Jump."

She did, and I caught her easily. Her arms went around my neck. She was crying, not making any sound but crying all the same. Her cheeks were wet.

I kissed her a couple of dozen times before I put her down. She was soft and warm and sweet and I suddenly felt like I was going to choke. My throat was all closed up and I couldn't say a word. I looked down at her and suddenly I saw that she was going to have a child.

I put my arms around her again, gently this time, scared to death that having her jump had hurt the baby she was carrying. My voice was a hoarse whisper more than it was a voice. "I didn't know. God, Julia, if I'd known I'd never have had you jump."

"It's all right, Jesse. It's all right!"

"No it isn't. Nothing's right. But I want you to know one thing. I didn't rob the bank in Fort Worth. And I didn't kill the banker."

"I knew you didn't, Jesse." She tried to sound confident but I detected a note of relief in her voice. Worriedly she said, "Jesse, there are two Pinkerton detectives in town waiting for you. They followed me from Fort Worth."

"I know. Grandpa told me."

"You can't stay, Jesse. You've got to go!"

"I had to see you. I had to know you were all right. I didn't want to leave you in Fort Worth but I didn't have a choice."

"I know, Jesse, and it's all right."

"But—"

She put a hand up and covered my mouth. "There's no time for things like that. There's only time for you and me."

"When's he due?"

"The baby? He's due almost any time. But how do you know it's going to be a boy?"

"I don't. I wouldn't care anyway. Why didn't you tell me? I'd never have let you jump."

She laughed softly. "I'd jump off a mountain if you were waiting to catch me."

I said, "Oh my God, Julia, what am I going to do?" All I wanted was Julia. All I wanted was to be with her and see my child born and hold him in my arms. I wanted to work like other men did and raise a family and . . .

I heard a door slam. I heard Mr. Delisa's harsh and ugly voice, "Get away from him, Julia. Get away from him!"

Her arms clutched me more tightly than before. "No, pa! No! If you're going to shoot him, then you'll have to shoot me too!"

I thought, *Oh God! I'm going to have to let him kill me or I'm going to have to kill him to save myself.*

I said, "I'm going, Mr. Delisa. Put down the gun and I'll go."

"The hell! You're a mad dog, Jesse, and you've hurt all of us enough! I'm going to end it now!"

I said, "I don't want to shoot you, Mr. Delisa, but I will if you force me to."

Julia said, "Jesse, no! You can't!"

A thousand-dollar reward, I thought cynically. That was all Julia's father wanted out of me. He was willing to kill me for that thousand-dollar reward.

Julia begged, "Jesse! Pa! Please don't do this. Please! Let him go, pa. Please let him go!"

A voice out in the darkness said, "Stand away from him, Mrs. Hand. Stand away from him and you won't get hurt."

It was a voice I didn't recognize. One of the Pinkerton detectives, I supposed. Then they *had* been alert, probably watching Julia's house in shifts throughout the night. They had known that sooner or later I would come.

With my left hand I pushed Julia behind me. With my right, I drew my gun. I didn't want to shoot anybody because doing so would draw their fire and endanger Julia, but neither was I going to let myself be shot or taken prisoner. I backed away into the darkness carefully. Frightened, Julia kept pace.

Mr. Delisa yelled, "Don't shoot, for God's sake! You might hit her!"

The Pinkerton man said, "He's not going to get away! I don't give a damn who *might* get hit!"

He fired and the bullet grazed my shoulder. Julia made a sound, a moan of terror and despair. I turned, giving her a push to make her fall. It was a chance I had to take. I didn't dare leave her stand with that Pinkerton man blasting away at me.

I ran toward the place I had left my horse, praying silently that the Pinkerton man hadn't found him before he managed to find me.

I reached my horse and mounted. I spurred savagely and thundered out of town.

XVII

UNTIL THAT night I had believed that somehow or other I was going to change. I was going to find a place somewhere and put away my gun and live down the things I had done. I figured I could even live down the false accusation in Fort Worth. I might have to change my name and appearance and I might have to go far away, but I had convinced myself that somehow I'd manage it.

That night, though, I faced the truth. I wasn't

going to change. Julia was lost to me and so was my child. Grandpa and Twin Forks and a normal life were also lost to me. I was what Hackett had made me, a gunman, a killer, as efficient and deadly as a rattlesnake. Hackett was dead and so was the man he had wanted killed, but I was still alive and would go on killing everyplace I went until I finally met someone who was faster than I was, or until I was captured by the Pinkertons. Or until the dueling code was outlawed in the West as it had already been outlawed in the East and South.

It scared me that the Pinkertons were after me. I guess everybody had heard stories about the Pinkertons. They never gave up no matter how long it took to get their man. With them after me I felt like I was living on borrowed time.

I pushed my horse pretty hard that night because I knew it wouldn't be hard to come by a fresh one when morning came. So that the Pinkerton men couldn't follow me by rail, I angled north. Maybe I'd go up into the Sioux country, I thought. Maybe that would be the only way I could shake them off. Maybe I'd even go to Canada.

In daylight, things began to look a little better than they had the night before. I began to try convincing myself again that I could change, that I could live down the past. I'd give myself the chance, I thought, just as soon as I got away from the Pinkertons. Maybe after two or three years people would forget about Jesse Hand. In that length of time my appearance would change a lot. I might even be able to get word to Julia and have her come to me.

In midmorning I reached a farm and managed to trade my horse for a fresh one. It cost me sixty dollars but money didn't matter any more. I had almost five hundred that I'd won. I could win more when it was gone.

Completely unfamiliar with the country ahead, I rode on, pushing the new horse as savagely as I had the one before. I traded again that evening and continued through the night, without pausing more than long enough to eat and rest the horse.

Farms were more scarce in the dry country through which I was now traveling. I figured Julesburg was somewhere south of me. I encountered small herds of buffalo every now and then, and sometimes saw pronghorned antelope, animals I had not seen before. They would stand on a hilltop in small bunches, staring at me curiously. When I drew near, they would turn and run with unbelievable speed.

In the river bottoms I would sometimes see a deer or two. I killed a young one on the third day and stopped long enough to build a fire, roast part of the deer and gorge myself on the meat.

Now, also, I occasionally came upon the camps of buffalo hunters, or upon solitary hunters riding across the plain. I avoided all contact with them because I didn't want anybody to be able to tell the Pinkertons I had passed this way. Once I hid in a dry wash for half an hour to avoid contact with a hunter angling toward me on a collision course.

I followed the Platte for a while, but I finally turned north just short of Fort Laramie. I'd been making good time and there had been heavy rains every afternoon for days. I figured it was safe to stop. The Pinkertons should have lost my trail a long ways back.

North of Fort Laramie by thirty or forty miles, I came to a ranch. I could tell by looking at it that it was a good-sized spread. It had a two-story frame ranch house and a barn about three times the size of the house, built of logs. There were maybe a dozen other buildings scattered around those two and there was a system of corrals almost as big as the shipping pens in Abilene.

I rode into the yard and half a dozen shepherd dogs ran out barking at me. Their tails were wagging too, so I dismounted and walked over to the kitchen door. I hadn't quite reached it when a voice yelled at me from the barn, "Hey! Over here!"

Something had made me take off my gun as I was riding in. Maybe I'd decided this would be a good place to try shaking off the past. I turned and walked to the man standing in the doorway of the barn. I said, "I'm Jim Harris, and I could use a job if you're hiring."

The man, who was near grandpa's age, looked at

me with narrowed eyes. He asked, "Know anything about cows?"

"A little."

He kept studying me until I wished he'd quit. He made me nervous. At last he said, "I can give you a line-shack job. It's hell for lonesome, though, and I don't want you taking off without telling anyone."

I said, "I'll stay. You can count on me."

He studied me for several minutes more. At last he nodded. "Thirty a month and keep. You ride straight north out of here for about twenty miles until you come to a wide dry creek. You follow that west for about another three-four miles and you'll see a little log shack with a tin roof on the north bank of the creek. That's the line shack. There's a man there now—Red Schickel. You tell him I said to stay there with you two or three days—long enough to show you what you're supposed to do. Then he can come on in."

I didn't want to seem dumb so I didn't ask what it was I was supposed to do. I thanked him and shook his hand and rode out. When I got about twenty miles north I found the dry creek and I followed that west until I came to the line shack. I saw a few cattle during the ride, which was almost thirty miles, but I saw no people and no signs of them.

It was getting dark when I reached the line shack. Smoke was coming out of a tin chimney and there was a lamp burning inside the place. A dog came out and barked at me and a few minutes later a man came to the door.

He was a Negro and the only red-headed Negro I'd ever seen. He was a great big man, taller than me and about thirty pounds heavier. He must have been forty, I supposed, and his hair wasn't bright red. It was a kind of dull copper shade.

I said, "You must be Red Schickel. I'm Jim Harris. The man back at the ranch south of here gave me a job. He said I was to tell you to show me what I'm supposed to do. Then he said you could come on in."

He stared at me for a long time. Finally he said in a voice as big as the rest of him, "All right, Jim. Get down and come inside. I got supper goin' here."

I got down and tied my horse to a rail. Red stuck out a hand and I took it. His hand seemed to wrap around mine, it was so big. I went inside. He had some meat frying on the top of the stove and some biscuits inside of it.

I'd known a few Negroes back home while I was growing up. They had always kept a line drawn between themselves and people who had white skins. Red was the first Negro I'd known who didn't act like there was a difference.

We sat down at a long, rough table and ate. Afterwards I carried water in from the trickle that rose in the dry creek bed not far from the cabin. While it heated, we sat and talked.

Red had sharp eyes. He saw the worn place on my pants leg where my gun holster had rubbed. He sized me up in other ways. It was like he knew what I was and what I'd done just by looking at me. As he poured hot water into a dishpan and tossed me a towel made from a flour sack, he said, "On the dodge, ain't you?"

I considered lying to him, then decided I wouldn't get away with it. I said, "Yes." I stared at him, somehow having the feeling he would understand. "I'm trying to get away from the past. It seemed like this might be a good place to start."

"Nothing wrong with that. Just so's you don't bring the past along with you. Just so's you don't start anything."

I promised I wouldn't and meant it. I didn't see how I could bring trouble to this lonely place. Red would leave in a couple of days and go back to the home place and I'd be left alone out here.

We finished the dishes. I went out and unsaddled my horse and put him into the corral. I gave him some hay and a little grain. Then I went back inside. I took the upper bunk and crawled up into it, but not before I'd got my gun out of the saddlebags and hung it from a nail within easy reach of my hand. That was instinct, I suppose. I didn't intend to wear the gun anymore but that didn't mean I had to be completely defenseless. Red stared at the gun and holster longer than seemed necessary, not missing the cut-down fast-drawn holster and the way the gun grips were worn from constant use.

I woke up a little before dawn like I always did. Red was already up, stirring around the stove getting a fire built. I dressed and put the gun back in my saddlebag. I said, "I'll get some wood."

I took the axe down from the nails on the wall and went outside. It was beginning to get light. Birds were chirping. There was a good clean smell in the air along with the smell of wood smoke from the stove. I walked down the stream a ways. A deer spooked out of the brush ahead of me and startled a bunch of cattle. They also trotted away. I found a dead tree and began to chop firewood. I worked steadily until I had a good-sized pile. I loaded up to carry it back to the cabin.

It took three trips but by the time I'd finished, Red had breakfast on. It consisted of flapjacks, fried side meat, fried venison, and sorghum for the flapjacks. He had coffee too.

I sat down and ate with him. We washed the dishes quickly afterward, but we still managed to get outside and saddled up by the time the sun poked above the eastern plain.

We rode out. Red said, "The ranch belongs to a man named Sauer and the brand is a Rafter S. This creek marks the northern boundary. Your job is to patrol this boundary, turning back all the Rafter S cattle that drift north of it."

"How—"

He grinned. "They won't hit the boundary on a dead run, boy. It ain't quite as hard as it might sound. You just ride back and forth along this creek, east one day and back, west the next day and back. You watch for tracks heading north. When you find fresh ones you follow and push the cattle that made 'em south for two or three miles or so."

That didn't sound very hard. He said, "We'll ride to the northeast corner today. We'll ride west tomorrow. After that you're on your own."

He kept his eyes on the ground. We hadn't gone more than two miles before he pointed out a trail to me. He said, "Prints are sharp: They ain't more'n half a day old. Besides, they wasn't here last time I was. So we'll follow 'em."

We turned north, following the trail. We'd ridden about half a mile when a small bunch of cattle got up in front of us. They'd been lying down.

Red and I circled around them and headed them back south. We crossed the creek, pushing them fairly hard, and kept on until they were two or three miles south of the line. After that we returned to the creek, turning east again when we came to it.

That day, we pushed three bunches of cattle back south of the line. The next day, riding west from the line shack, we didn't find any trails.

In camp that night Red said, "The thing that will kill you is the lonesomeness. But if you can stand that you'll be all right. I'll be back with supplies in a couple of weeks."

I said, "If anybody comes snooping around looking for me, will you let me know?"

"I'll let you know."

He rode away toward the south. I had a strange feeling that he really would let me know if anyone came looking for me, no matter what they told him I had done.

I built a fire in the stove and cooked my supper and then went to bed. Next day I began the deadly routine of the line-rider's job.

It didn't seem deadly to me and for a change I was glad to be alone. But before a week had passed, I was down below the cabin in the creek bottom practicing my draw and shooting at tin cans. It was all right to put away the gun, I told myself, but that didn't mean I had to forget all that I had learned. Besides, it would help to pass the time.

The Pinkerton men might show up any day. Some local gunslick might find out I was working out on Rafter S. Some friend or relative of someone I'd killed might show up looking for my scalp.

I suppose I deserve all the things that have happened to me. I guess I never really wanted to give up the gun at all. If I had I'd have thrown it down a well some place where I couldn't find it again.

XVIII

LINE RIDING wasn't particularly hard work but I was in the saddle at dawn and lots of days I didn't get back to the cabin until after dark. One day I began to carry my gun again. I didn't see how it could do any harm and I didn't want to get caught without it if somebody rode by and happened to recognize me. Besides, I was putting in such long hours that I never got a chance to practice with it any more. If I kept it with me I figured I could get in a little practice while I was resting my horse at noon.

Red returned in two weeks driving a wagon loaded with supplies for me and with hay and grain for my horse. He also brought along an extra horse so that I'd have a fresh one to ride every day. As soon as the wagon was unloaded, he headed back toward the home place. He said that a bunch of homesteaders were coming out the next day with a man from the government land office to see Mr. Sauer. They were complaining that they ought to be allowed to file homestead claims on Rafter S. Naturally Mr. Sauer didn't agree. He'd settled on the land when nobody else wanted it and he'd fought Indians to hold onto it. Besides, he claimed, nobody could raise crops on it. The homesteaders would get starved out but by the time they were, they'd already have ruined a lot of land, plowing and building fences and shacks that would have to be torn down before the land could go back to grass again.

I didn't know much about Mr. Sauer. I'd only met him once, But he had seemed like a decent, reasonable man.

The day after Red brought the supplies, I stopped at noon in a little grove of scrubby trees where there was a trickle of water for my horse. I watered and unsaddled him and staked him out to graze. I walked downstream a ways to practice with my gun. I practiced my draw for twenty or thirty minutes and then fired about a dozen rounds at a target, drawing the gun for every shot.

I had just finished when I got the sudden, uneasy feeling that I was not alone. I glanced around and saw a couple of wagons halted on the north side of the creek. The people in the wagons were watching me.

I holstered my gun and walked toward them but they turned their wagons and drove hurriedly away. Since I didn't have my horse handy, I didn't try to follow and talk to them.

I didn't think much about it. I went on about my business, riding east one day and west the next, switching horses every day. I guess about a week passed. Then one evening about dusk I rode in to the clearing that held the cabin and found Mr. Sauer and Red and two other men waiting there for me.

Mr. Sauer said, "This is Jim Harris, gentlemen."

I got down off my horse. One of the strangers had a star on his vest. I didn't offer to shake hands. I just stood there waiting for them to tell me what this was all about.

Mr. Sauer said, "Jim, a couple of wagonloads of nesters ran into you the other day. They caught you practicing with your gun. They said they'd never seen anyone so fast and they complained to Mr. Shattuck here that I was hiring gunfighters to frighten them off land claimed by Rafter S."

I looked at the man he'd indicated. I said, "I was hired to ride line and nothing else."

The man with the star was looking carefully at me. He asked, "How old are you?"

I said, "Eighteen."

"Ever been in Fort Worth?"

Something seemed to grab me by the throat for an instant and I guess my answer didn't get out quite fast enough. "No. Why?"

"You fit the description of Jesse Hand. He's wanted for murder and bank robbery in Fort Worth."

I didn't say anything. The man said, "Jim Harris, huh? Same initials as Jesse Hand. I've never seen it fail. When a man changes his name, he sticks to the same initials he had before."

I said, "I never heard of Jesse Hand. My name's Jim Harris."

The man was studying the way I wore my gun.

He was also studying my face. Why, I wondered, hadn't I had sense enough to leave the gun in my saddlebags? If those two wagonloads of home-steaders hadn't caught me practicing with it, if they hadn't seen how fast I was with it, they'd never have complained about me to Shattuck, and he'd never have relayed their complaints to the sheriff and to Mr. Sauer.

Sauer looked at Shattuck. "What do you want me to do? I don't want you and those homesteaders thinking that I'm acting in bad faith, or that I'm hiring gunfighters to frighten them."

"Then get rid of him."

"That's hardly fair to him. He's been doing his work and he hasn't bothered anyone."

"He can get another job."

I said, "I don't want another job. I want this one."

The sheriff said, "All right. Let him stay as long as he behaves himself."

I glanced at the lawman. His face was hard and his eyes were as cold as bits of stone. I suddenly knew why he was advising Shattuck to let me stay. He thought I was Jesse Hand but he wasn't certain enough to take action now. He just wanted me around long enough for him to go back to town and check the description on the wanted poster from Fort Worth. He also wanted men to back him up in case I turned out to be Jesse Hand.

Shattuck agreed grudgingly. He and the sheriff

mounted and headed away into the darkness. Mr. Sauer seemed relieved that he didn't have to fire me. He followed. Red started to ride after him but I called, "Red."

He turned and came riding back. I said, "I've got to leave, Red, but I don't want to tell Mr. Sauer in front of those other men."

He didn't say anything. He just sat on his horse looking down at me. It was so dark I couldn't see his expression. He said, "I'll tell him for you, Jesse. What about your pay?"

"Maybe I'll ride by the home place and pick it up tomorrow." But I knew that I would not. I was going to put as much distance as I could between myself and this place tonight because tomorrow the sheriff would be out here with a posse looking for me. He'd probably send off wires to the Pinkertons tonight.

I watched Red ride away. Maybe I'd been a fool to trust him, I thought as he and the others faded out of sight. Maybe he'd tell Sauer and Shattuck and the sheriff who I was and they'd turn around and come back for me.

I went into the line shack and gathered up my things. Fortunately my own horse wasn't the one I had been riding that day. My horse was standing in the corral. I saddled him and tied on my blanket roll and saddlebags. I didn't even wait long enough to eat.

I rode away, angry and bitter because of the way

this had turned out. I kept telling myself it wasn't my fault but down deep I knew it was. I'd never be able to get and hold an honest job until I was willing to throw away my gun. And if I did throw it away I'd leave myself defenseless against the Pinkertons and against the law and against anyone else that might happen to recognize me.

Out of my bitterness that night came a decision. If I couldn't live without my gun, then I'd have to learn to live with it. I'd earn my living using it.

I covered close to fifty miles that night. I covered another fifty the next day before I stopped to rest.

That fall and winter were aimless months for me. I was on the move practically all the time. I went south into New Mexico and Arizona and into the Texas panhandle and even farther south than that. I'd stay in a town two or three weeks and then I'd leave. Money didn't seem to be much of a problem for me, thanks to the skill with cards that I had learned. But I didn't like gambling. I liked to be outdoors. I wanted another riding job like the one I'd had on Rafter S. Besides, living around saloons and gambling inevitably led to gunfights. I found out that there were a lot of bad losers in the world.

More and more the name of Jesse Hand became known. I was credited in one town with having killed twenty men. It was twenty-three in another. The number seemed to grow with the telling.

Plenty of lawmen recognized my name and knew I was wanted in Fort Worth for murder and bank robbery. None of them seemed anxious to try collecting the reward but I had to stay on guard anyway, because I knew if they thought they could get away with it they'd gun me down like a rabid dog. I also knew I had to keep moving or the Pinkertons would catch up with me.

In April I rode into Denver and gawked like a farm boy at the tall buildings and busy streets. It was the biggest city I had ever seen. I put up at a hotel and took my horse to a stable, and set out afoot to see the sights.

I hit the fanciest saloon I saw and ordered beer. I was standing there drinking it and staring at a painting of a pink naked woman behind the bar when a man stepped up beside me. He said, "Can I buy you a drink?"

I turned my head and looked at him. He was a little younger than Mr. Sauer had been but not very much. He was dressed like a cowman but anyone could tell his clothes had cost a lot. He had on the fanciest pair of boots I ever saw. He laid a twenty-dollar gold piece on the bar.

I said, "I've got a drink." I was trying to figure out who he was and what he wanted with me. He wasn't a Pinkerton detective. They don't dress like that. He said, "I'm just trying to be agreeable."

I nodded. "All right. I'll have another beer." I picked up my glass and finished it.

He signaled the bartender, who brought me another beer. He brought the stranger a bottle and a glass. The man poured himself a drink. He seemed hesitant about getting out what was on his mind, but at last he said, "I have a ranch a hundred miles northwest of Cheyenne. I'm hiring in case you'd be interested."

I said, "Gunhands or cowhands?"

I guess he hadn't expected me to be so blunt. He looked a little flustered but he said, "Gunhands. Nesters are moving in and they're robbing me and my neighbors blind."

"What about the pay?"

"Two hundred a month. An extra two hundred if you have to kill anyone."

That sounded pretty cold-blooded to me, that two hundred bonus for every one I killed. It was like putting a bounty on the nesters' heads. But I'd been drifting long enough. I wanted to settle down for a while. I said, "What if it was to turn out I was wanted by the law?"

"I can guarantee the sheriff won't bother you. He's an Association man. And I doubt if any outside lawmen are going to risk trying to take you off my place."

I figured he ought to know all of it. "Not even the Pinkertons?"

"Not even the Pinkertons. You give me your loyalty and I'll give you mine."

I nodded. "All right. When do we leave?"

"Tomorrow morning. I have four other men. We'll meet in front of this saloon at dawn."

I stuck out my hand and he took it. I told him I was Jesse Hand and he said he was Al Flack. He finished his drink and left.

I spent the rest of the day wandering around town looking at the sights. I turned in early but half an hour before dawn I was dressed and on my way out of the hotel. I got my horse at the livery stable and reached the saloon where Al Flack had said we'd meet. I was early so I sat down on the edge of the boardwalk and waited. After a while the others began to show up. I didn't know any of them but they all had the same look about them, the well-used guns, the watchfulness as though they didn't dare trust anybody. Two of them had a mean look and I disliked them instantly. I suddenly felt glad I wasn't one of the nesters Flack was trying to get off his ranch.

Flack showed up, driving a buggy, and led out, heading north. We followed the river along the stage road. Flack said we could get breakfast at a stagecoach way station about ten miles north of town.

Riding behind the buggy, we introduced ourselves. One reminded me of Hackett. He was medium-sized and middle-aged. He wore a small mustache and his hair was gray and long on his neck and around his ears. He looked as if he'd be very competent with the gun he wore, but I doubted if he was as fast as me. His name was

Billings. Nathan Billings. And he didn't want anyone to call him Nate.

Another was a red-haired man that I'd have said was twenty-five. He said his name was Ed Widemeier. He had big freckles on a face that was red from exposure to the sun. His hands also had big freckles on the back. He wore his gun differently from the others, in a special holster made to fit into his hip pocket. Because of it, he rode his horse in an awkward, twisted position so that he wouldn't have to sit on it.

The two I didn't like were as different as night from day. One was tall and thin and pale, with hair almost the color of a mouse's hair and just as fine. He had pale, washed-out blue eyes and a thin, almost colorless mouth that managed to stay hidden most of the time beneath a sweeping mustache the color of his hair. He said his name was Laramie, and that was all the name he gave.

The last was a slight, dark-skinned man who gave his name as Domingo Garcia. He was quick and nervous with his hands, which were as pale and finely made as Julia's hands had been. He carried a smaller gun than the rest of us, a .38 caliber like mine but not nearly as big as mine. He reminded me of a bright and deadly snake that will strike at anything that comes in range.

Garcia and Laramie seemed to like each other, though they didn't talk very much. They just rode side by side behind the buggy. Billings and

Widemeier and I rode farther back, far enough to be out of the buggy's dust.

I knew what I had become. There was no longer any use telling myself I was going to change and give it up. I wasn't. I'd be a hired gun until it was time for me to die. I was like these others, my only function in life being to kill for a price.

XIX

South Central Wyoming, I discovered, was much like the eastern part. It was grassland, dotted with clumps of scrub sagebrush and in places, where the land was poor, with a plant called greasewood that cattle would eat when there was nothing else. Bluffs rose out of the plain in the distance, their faces of gray sandstone, and the land was crisscrossed by dry washes cut by the sudden rush of water from cloudbursts that plagued the country in summertime.

Antelope were numerous and sometimes we saw a few scattered buffalo. As in eastern Wyoming, where Mr. Sauer lived, the land had first been settled entirely by cattlemen. Ranch houses were built where there was water and each cattleman held at least as much land as he could see from his house. Sometimes his land stretched away as far as a cow could walk for water in a day. Most of the ranches were at least five or six miles across.

The wind never stopped blowing. It made the

grass ripple until it looked like waves. In this part of Wyoming, as in the eastern part, a change was taking place. Settlers, who had started moving west after the Civil War, were now reaching here, settling along the streams and beside the springs. They were backed by the United States Government. The cowmen had no title to the lands they held, said the government. The immigrants had the right to file on it.

Some cowmen, like Mr. Sauer, were reasonable and did not actively dispute that right. They discouraged settlement but they did nothing to prevent it, even though they knew the settlers stole and ate their beef.

Others, like Flack, met the settlers with violence. They formed associations like the Wyoming Cattlemen's Association and the Colorado Stockgrowers Association. They hired experts to do their fighting and killing for them.

I was one of the experts.

We traveled steadily northward for four days, covering about fifty miles a day. The second day we left the South Platte, which we had followed north out of Denver. The third day we crossed the Laramie River in the morning and the North Platte in the afternoon. On the fourth day we arrived at Flack's Wagon Wheel Ranch.

It was late when we arrived, so we turned in right away. Flack had a bunkhouse big enough for twenty men. There were only a couple of empty bunks.

We got up at dawn and, dressed and washed, gathered at the cookshack to eat. When that was over with, Flack and his foreman stood in front of the cookshack and handed out jobs to the regular hands for the day.

I knew this wasn't the entire crew. Some of the men were probably in town. Others were riding line, as I had done on Rafter S. The crew went out, got their horses and began to saddle up. Flack introduced his foreman, a bull-shouldered man of about thirty-five, with skin like leather and eyes that looked us over with plain contempt. Flack said, "This is Donovan. He's foreman here. He speaks for me so you'll take his orders just like you'd take mine."

He waited a moment for that to sink in. Then he said, "Donovan is going to take the bunch of you for a ride. You're going to visit all the settlers so they can get a look at you. We'll first give them a chance to get off my land peaceably."

The alternative was plain enough. If they did not get off, we'd go to work and start to earn our pay.

We went to the corral, caught fresh horses and saddled up. Donovan did likewise. He was curt and unsmiling with us and I could feel antagonism building up in Widemeier and Billings. Garcia and Laramie didn't seem to mind.

We rode out. Flack's ranch had a creek running

through it named Cut Nose Creek. Flack's was one of the bigger spreads. It stretched along Cut Nose Creek for about twelve miles. Flack claimed a strip of land five miles on both sides of the creek. That meant his ranch contained a hundred and twenty sections; it was ten miles wide and twelve miles long.

Settlers had taken up quarter sections all along Cut Nose Creek. If they were allowed to stay, it meant that eventually Flack would have nothing left. He didn't even own the land he'd built his house and other buildings on.

Donovan explained the situation to us as we rode. So far, only a small portion of Cut Nose Creek had been filed on. But if the settlers already here were allowed to stay, it was only a matter of time until others would come and claim the rest.

Flack had no sympathy for them. He'd worked hard for years and had put a good part of his life into making something of this land. He had risked his life a dozen times doing it. He had raised his family here.

Now a bunch of squatters from the East threatened to take it all away from him. I didn't blame him for fighting back. I figured any man would have fought.

The first of the shacks we came to was built out of railroad ties. The roof was flat, made of sod still too new to have weeds growing out of it. There was a small barbed-wire corral. About an acre of grass had been broken with a plow but it hadn't been planted yet. A milk cow and a mule stood in the corral.

A woman was hanging clothes out on a line. A man with a week's growth of whiskers was mending harness beside a lean-to that was attached to the house.

Three small, dirty children were playing in the yard. A boy of about twelve was trying to repair one of the plowhandles with strips of rawhide he had soaked in a rusty pail full of water.

All of them just looked at us. I hoped the rest of the settlers had more spirit than this outfit had. Donovan rode in, followed by the rest of us. I saw the terror that came suddenly into the woman's face, the sullenness that touched the man's, the defiance that showed in the young boy's eyes. Donovan didn't waste any time. He said harshly, "Be gone by this time tomorrow. We're coming to burn your house and tear your fences down. If you're gone when we get here, nobody will get hurt."

The man's voice had a whiny quality. "You got no right. The gov'mint—"

"The hell with the government. You be gone tomorrow." Donovan turned his horse and rode away.

We rode on down the stream. That first one was the sorriest bunch we saw. Some of the houses were bigger and more permanent. Some of the settlers were cowmen rather than farmers. Donovan said some of them ran as many as twenty cows.

None of the men were as whiny and defeated as the first had been. Several met us with shotguns in their hands. Donovan's warning was the same to all of them. They had until tomorrow. Flack was through coddling them. It was leave or get burned out. If they fought back they would be killed.

It was noon by the time we had visited them all. We returned by another route. Once, when we rode close enough to Cut Nose Creek, I saw three men galloping along the creek. They were getting together, I supposed, trying to organize so that they could resist. Not that resisting would do them any good. Flack had hired us to see that nobody refused to leave.

There was a brief moment when I didn't feel very proud. Then I began to make excuses to myself. If Flack hadn't found me, he'd have found somebody else. What was going to happen here tomorrow would happen whether I was part of it or not. It was the times that were to blame. Conflict between cultivated land and free grass was natural. The cowmen would probably remain but they were going to have to legally acquire the land.

In the meantime they would try holding on by force. I had expected to go the following day, but Donovan told us we were going to wait. Waiting would worry the settlers. Those who intended to stay had probably banded together to resist. There was no hurry to burn the houses of those who had decided to leave. That made sense. Donovan didn't want war, which was what he would have had if he'd followed through on the day following his first visit to the settlers. He knew they couldn't stay forted up forever. Sooner or later they'd have to scatter again to their own homes. When they did, we would descend on them.

The five of us loafed around the bunkhouse. We played poker most of the time, and most of the time I won. I wasn't fool enough to use the card tricks I knew. Not with this bunch. Not unless I wanted to shoot it out with those that lost. I just won because I knew how to play the game and maybe because I didn't care whether I won or not.

I couldn't help comparing this kind of life with what I'd had with Julia the short time we'd been together. The comparison showed me plainly how empty this life was. The only thing that made it bearable at all, I realized, was the excitement, the danger of it.

We stayed at Wagon Wheel a week. At the end of the week, Donovan split us into two groups. He started Widemeier and me at the upper end of Cut Nose Creek. He sent Garcia, Laramie and Billings to the other end.

The tie shack was still there. The milk cow was still in the corral. The boy was plowing with the mule.

We rode in toward the house. The kids saw us and ran for it. I caught a glimpse of the woman's dress as she slammed the door. When we were about a hundred yards away, a shotgun boomed.

I glanced at the boy out in the field. He had unhitched the mule. He was on the animal's back, kicking him in the ribs, heading downstream toward the nearest of the other settlers.

Widemeier said harshly, "I'll stop that kid! You take care of this!"

He turned his horse and pounded after the boy. His horse was faster than the boy's plow mule, and he began to overtake him rapidly. From where I was I could see the boy had some kind of gun, but whether it was a shotgun or rifle I couldn't tell.

And suddenly I knew I was standing at a crossroads. I hadn't chosen this time and place for a decision; it had chosen me. Widemeier would kill that boy because the boy had a gun and would probably try to defend himself with it. If I stayed here and did nothing to stop it, I would be as guilty as Widemeier was.

I whirled my horse and spurred after Widemeier. Killing is one thing when your antagonist is capable of killing you, or is a rustler. But a twelve-year-old boy . . . I'd come a long way, but I hadn't come that far.

Ahead of me, Widemeier was now less than two hundred yards behind the boy. I was a quarter-mile farther back. I yelled at Widemeier but he didn't hear. And the boy, completely terrified, turned in his saddle and fired.

The gun puffed smoke. By now Widemeier had closed the gap between him and the boy to fifty yards. The boy's gun puffed smoke again. I supposed it was a double barreled shotgun, which meant it now was empty.

Widemeier drew and raised his gun. Smoke puffed from it. The boy toppled sideways out of his saddle and hit the ground rolling. He raised a little cloud of dust and then laid still.

My chest felt empty. My stomach churned and I felt like vomiting. I reached Widemeier, who sat his saddle looking down at the boy, calmly ejecting the empty from his gun, as calmly replacing it. I said, "You dirty sonofabitch, you didn't have to kill the kid!"

He swung his head, his eyes blazing. His gun was in his hand and I knew he'd use it, but I waited until it began to come up, until the intention was there plainly in his eyes. Then I drew my own gun and fired.

He fired almost simultaneously and his bullet, deflected at the last instant by a frightened movement of his horse, plowed into my thigh, tearing through flesh and exiting from my rump. It was like I'd sat down on a red-hot stove.

My bullet hit him squarely in the middle of the forehead and knocked him bodily backward over his horse's rump. He hit the ground less than three feet from the dead boy, and he never moved again.

I slid off my horse. Blood was streaming down my leg. I ran for a clump of brush and threw up. When I straightened, drenched with sweat and half-blind with pain, I knew finally what I had to do.

I'd report to Donovan and tell him what had happened and what I had done. I'd see a doctor in the nearest town about my leg.

But after that, I was going south. I was going to stop running from that false charge of bank robbery and murder in Fort Worth. And the only way to stop running away from it was to go there, face it, and either prove I didn't do it or get hanged.

I won't say I wasn't scared. Thought of a hangman's noose made me break out in a clammy sweat. But I stood at a crossroads and the other road was even worse.

XX

BOTH DONOVAN and Flack were appalled at what Widemeier had done. They hadn't really wanted anyone to get killed, least of all a twelve-year-old boy. They called off the sweep along Cut Nose Creek immediately. Flack told me to go to bed and sent to Laramie for a doctor.

I waited until the doctor came. He trimmed the ragged flesh where the bullet had exited from my rump and sewed up the wound. He bandaged me and gave me some laudanum for the pain.

That night I got out of bed, dressed, and limped to the corral, carrying my saddle. I caught my horse, saddled, mounted and rode out heading south. I was afraid if I laid around until that wound healed, the horror of what had happened would fade from my mind. I was afraid my determination would fade with it, afraid I'd never go to Fort Worth at all.

I admitted that there was a good chance the people in Fort Worth would string me up from the nearest tree without even listening to what I had to say. But at that point in my life, even death seemed preferable to going on the way I was. Sooner or later, I'd get like Widemeier had been. I'd be willing to kill a twelve-year-old boy to earn the money that was being paid for my gun.

Moreover, it was only a matter of time until I turned outlaw. A man might start out just being good with a gun, just defending his own life with it. But there were always successive steps, steps I was beginning to see more clearly than I ever had before. The first I had already taken. I had hired out my gun. Next, I would become a paid assassin. And lastly, I would become an outlaw.

The first thing I did was to put the gun and belt in my saddlebag. I figured it was a way I could prove my good faith to myself. But I won't pretend

I didn't waver. I wavered fifty times a day. But something kept me going on, traveling slowly south across the vast high plains.

Every day and every night I thought of Julia, and I thought of my son, who would have been born by now. When I wavered, I told myself that if I didn't go through with it, I'd never see him. I'd never see Julia again.

I avoided towns as much as possible. I stayed clear of Cheyenne and of Denver. I bought supplies at stagecoach way stations along the way and I stayed out of saloons where I might be recognized. I let my beard grow even though it was thin and raggedy.

I took Uncle Dick Wootton's toll road across Raton Pass and turned east. My horse went lame and I traded him but I never stopped for more than a night. It seemed like I'd been traveling forever. I was dirty and thin, having lost a lot of weight because of the wound, and sometimes, even after weeks of traveling, my leg would ache so much I'd think I couldn't ride another mile.

But it seemed like there was a fire in me now, a fire that wouldn't die. Something beyond myself kept me going on. Something I didn't understand was forcing me and I couldn't have stopped if I'd wanted to.

I came into Fort Worth in early evening. I waited in the same mesquite thicket where Julia and I had camped so long ago until it got completely dark.

Then I rode into town, staying on the backstreets, so I would not be seen.

I didn't know who I ought to see. Not the sheriff, certainly. The only one I knew who might believe me was Mrs. Ferguson. I figured maybe if I could convince her I hadn't done what they said I had, she'd get somebody to talk to me and listen to what I had to say. Maybe a judge or magistrate.

I reached the house where she had lived. I tied my horse in the alley and limped stiffly to her back door, leaving my gun in my saddlebags. I had hesitated over that but I finally admitted that if I carried the gun I might use it. And if I did, there would be no chance ever again of clearing up the murder and bank robbery charge.

There was a lamp burning in the kitchen. I peered in the window before I knocked. Mrs. Ferguson was alone, and she came to the door immediately. She stared at me without recognition until I said, "It's Jesse Hand, Mrs. Ferguson. I've come back to try and prove I didn't rob the bank."

She stiffened when she heard my name. For just an instant she looked scared. Then she said practically, "Well, if you'd done it, I doubt if you'd come back here trying to prove you didn't. Come on in, son. You look like you're half starved to death."

I went in. I sank down in a chair, beat and weak now that I'd got where I was going. She put some coffee in front of me and began to fix me something to eat. I said, "I never thanked you for taking care of Julia. I never got a chance. But I'm grateful, ma'am. I'm mighty obliged."

She put some food in front of me. "Eat. We'll talk afterward."

I ate. When I had finished she said, "They'll lynch you. I'm not even sure the sheriff could hold them off."

I said, "I don't want to see the sheriff, ma'am. The night the bank was robbed, I was down at the livery stable selling a horse to the liveryman. I thought I heard a shot, and I looked up in the direction the sound came from. I saw the sheriff come out of the bank. I figure he had to be the one who killed the banker and robbed the place. He put it on me because I'd been in the bank earlier to ask for a job. I guess I scared that banker some."

"I could get the judge."

"Yes ma'am."

She got her hat and a shawl and put them on. She went out into the night.

She was gone about twenty minutes, I suppose. When she came back, she was out of breath and so excited she could hardly talk. She said, "You've got to run, Jesse. The judge refused to talk to you until the sheriff had you locked up in jail. He's gone after the sheriff now."

I got to my feet. I started for the back door. Before I reached it, I heard a shout out in the yard, "Hand! Give yourself up! If you don't we're coming in!"

I didn't recognize the voice, but that wasn't surprising. I didn't know anyone in Fort Worth. Mrs. Ferguson said, "I'm sorry, Jesse. I didn't know the judge would refuse to talk to you."

"Who's that yelling?"

"The sheriff, Sam Gould."

I had a sinking feeling in my stomach. I'd left my gun in my saddlebags and I was defenseless without it. They'd take me, alive or dead. And if the sheriff was the one who had killed the banker and robbed the bank, he'd see to it that I never lived to get to trial. I'd either be killed in an escape attempt or he'd turn me over to a mob.

I said, "Tell them I surrender. Make them come in after me. At least that way I won't get shot the minute I step out the door."

Mrs. Ferguson went to the door. "Sheriff?"

"What?"

"He's unarmed. He says he'll surrender, but he don't want to come out for fear he'll be shot."

"Well I ain't coming in. How do I know he ain't got a gun on you making you say that?"

"You know it because I'm telling you," she said sharply.

"Send him out. That's the only way."

Mrs. Ferguson called, "Judge?"

"What?"

"Come in and take him prisoner."

The sheriff said, "Don't do it, judge. It's a trick. He'll put a gun on you and use you for a hostage."

Mrs. Ferguson said, "Judge, he came back to Fort Worth of his own free will. He says the sheriff will kill him the minute he comes out the door."

I heard the judge's voice, but I couldn't make out what he said. A few minutes later, though, he came in through the back door, timidly as if he thought he was going to get shot.

I stood in the middle of the kitchen, holding my hands out away from my body so he could see I didn't have a gun. I said, "Judge, I never robbed that bank. I only asked the banker for a job. I guess I scared him, though, because as soon as I left, he went after the sheriff. I was down in the livery stable selling a horse when I heard what sounded like a shot. I looked up the street and saw the sheriff coming out of the bank alone."

The judge stared at me for a long time, and I didn't let my eyes waver. At last he nodded. "All right. Come on. You'll have to go to jail, but I'll check your story out."

I followed him out the door. There were a lot of men in Mrs. Ferguson's back yard. One of them yelled, "Let's string the sonofabitch up right now! No use payin' for the cost of a trial. He's guilty. John Rafferty said it was him before he died."

John Rafferty must have been the banker who had been killed. I said, "Who did he say that to?"

"To the sheriff. He died before the sheriff could get the doc for him."

I turned my head and looked at the judge. He

said, "I'm not going to try this case here in Mrs. Ferguson's back yard." He glanced at the sheriff, "Take him down and lock him up. I'm going to hold you responsible."

The sheriff scowled, "What do you mean, you're going to hold me responsible?"

"For his safety. He says you killed John Rafferty. He says you robbed the bank."

"Why the lyin' sonofabitch! I'll teach him—"

The judge said, "I told you I'd hold you responsible and I will. Now take him down and lock him up."

It sounded like the judge wasn't going to go. Gould had a shotgun jammed against my spine and I knew I was never going to reach the jail. I looked at the judge and there must have been panic in my eyes. The judge said, "It's all right, son."

I said, "The hell it is! Do you really think I'll ever reach that jail?"

"He won't hurt you. He knows he'll answer to me if he does."

"Answer for what? For shooting a prisoner tryin' to escape? That's better than answering for bank robbery and murder, ain't it?"

The shotgun dug viciously into my back and I grunted with the pain. The sheriff snarled, "Shut up, you!" I heard the hammer click as he cocked the gun.

And suddenly I knew what he was going to do. He was going to shove me and make it look like I had tried to run. Just as soon as the judge left, that was what he was going to do.

I yelled, "Judge, ask the liveryman! He'll tell you he paid me forty dollars for my horse! Why would I be selling a horse if I'd just robbed the bank?"

There was quiet now in the yard. Several of the men were staring hard at Sam Gould's face. Someone said, "Sam bought his ranch right after this kid was supposed to have robbed the bank."

Sam Gould yelled, "What the hell do you mean by that? I'd been savin' that money for years."

I felt his muscles tense and knew my time had come. He'd already let me talk too much and he wasn't going to let me talk any more. With me dead, trying to escape, he might convince them that I was the one who had robbed the bank. If he let me live, the doubts I had started were going to grow and grow until it was him who went to the gallows instead of me.

I felt his big hand against my back. He probably figured that when he pushed me I'd try to stay on my feet. I'd stagger away and it would look like I was trying to run away.

He pushed, hard, but instead of trying to keep my feet, I let myself fall deliberately. I hit the ground not six feet away from him and I laid there still, knowing it was my only chance. If I rolled, or tried to get up, he'd cut me in two. Maybe he would anyway but it was the chance I had to take.

Lying prone, and motionless, I held my hands partway up, palms spread to show I didn't have anything in them. I saw the twin bores of that shotgun and I saw the murderous expression in the sheriff's eyes. I heard the judge yell, "Sam! Don't shoot!"

But I knew the sheriff was going to shoot and I knew I'd gambled with my life and lost. I saw the tightening of the muscles around his eyes. I waited for the charge to tear into me.

Movement behind the sheriff caught my eyes. It was the old judge. He reached the sheriff just as the shotgun roared. He struck the sheriff from behind, throwing off his aim enough so that the full charge went into the ground a foot to one side of me. A few pellets burned my leg, but that was all.

I didn't wait for the second charge. I came to my hands and knees and plunged toward the sheriff. I came up beneath the shotgun, forcing the muzzle skyward. It roared a second time. This charge tore harmlessly through a tree directly overhead. Leaves and twigs began sifting to the ground before the smoke had cleared.

I was no match for the sheriff physically. He yanked the gun away and took a swing at me with it. But now the judge's voice had steel in it, and a rifle was in his hands. "Sam! Drop it or I'll kill you! Believe me, Sam! I will!"

I knew that I had won. The judge and several others had taken a stand and because they had, I was still alive. Later I found out that a ranch wasn't the only thing the sheriff had bought after the bank robbery. He'd bought a team of high-stepping horses and a rig. He'd bought cattle and he'd bought a lot of things for his wife. When the townspeople started remembering all the things that he had bought, they'd known that what I said was true.

I stayed at Mrs. Ferguson's that night and the sheriff stayed in a cell down at the jail. In the morning, the judge gave me a paper that said I had been cleared of the murder and bank robbery charge.

I dug the gun out of my saddlebags. I gave it to the judge. "I won't be needing that. I'm going home."

I rode out, heading north. It wasn't going to be easy and I knew that it was not. The people back in Twin Forks weren't going to let me live there in peace. They weren't going to forget, either what my father had done or what I had done.

But there had to be a place for Julia and me and our son. Somewhere there had to be a place. We'd keep looking until we found it. Sooner or later maybe everybody would just forget there had ever been a man named Jesse Hand who was handy with a gun.

I had a new chance, one I'd stopped thinking I would get. I was determined not to spoil it because of bitterness about the past. Maybe the people in Twin Forks hadn't helped me when I needed help. But the people in Fort Worth had.

I kicked my horse into a lope, remembering Julia now and wondering if my son would look like me. And I realized that for the first time in months I was grinning. I was grinning like a doggoned fool.

Center Point Publishing
600 Brooks Road • PO Box 1
Thorndike ME 04986-0001 USA

(207) 568-3717

US & Canada:
1 800 929-9108
www.centerpointlargeprint.com